CW00430071

The Mosaic Murders

Mysteries of Lavender Lane, Volume 3

S.R. Moore

Published by S.R. Moore, 2024.

This is a work of fiction. Similarities to real people, places, or events are entirely coincidental.

THE MOSAIC MURDERS

First edition. March 27, 2024.

Copyright © 2024 S.R. Moore.

ISBN: 979-8224507641

Written by S.R. Moore.

Also by S.R. Moore

Table of Contents

Shadows and Tesserae: Unraveling the Mystery of Lavender Lane

IN THE PICTURESQUE and peaceful neighborhood of Lavender Lane, the day dawned with a deceptive calmness. The morning light filtered through the ancient trees, creating a beautiful display of shadows and highlights on the cobblestone paths. Jane, who had a great appreciation for ancient mosaics, strolled down the street, her steps blending harmoniously with the melodies of the morning birds. Every step she took felt like a silent conversation with the past, as she traced the intricate patterns on the cobblestones, imagining the countless stories they held.

This town, composed of the interwoven cobblestone paths and ivy-covered buildings, seemed to hold secrets from times long gone, beckoning the curious and the brave to listen. The gentle rustling of the ivy, caressed by a soft breeze, created a soothing lullaby. Bathed in the golden morning light, the weathered walls stood as silent guardians of history.

Lost in thought, Jane mused softly, her voice blending with the surroundings. "Lavender Lane, a place where history and the present gracefully dance together. Yet today, the stage seems to have been veiled, tainted by a more eerie presence." Her words lingered in the air, reflecting the tension between the lane's beauty and the unspoken uneasiness that seemed to lurk beneath the surface.

Upon entering her beloved café, a symphony of familiar sounds greeted Jane—the cheerful jingle of the doorbell, which always announced her arrival like an old friend; the comforting murmur of early customers engaged in whispered conversations and soft laughter, knitting together a sense of community and warmth; and the enchanting aroma of freshly brewed coffee, promising a momentary respite from the mysteries that awaited outside. In the early hours, the café, with its warmth and familiarity, possessed an almost magical quality, its windows frosted with the breath of those seeking solace within its embrace.

Mrs. Dalloway, the café's owner, welcomed Jane with a smile as warm as the beverages she served. Her smile, a beacon in the cozy atmosphere, exuded a feeling of home and comfort. "Jane, my dear, the usual?" she asked with a soothing voice, gracefully beginning to prepare Jane's favorite drink. The clinking of cups and the hissing of the espresso machine added rhythm to their morning routine, a melody of familiarity and solace that starkly contrasted with the whispered secrets of Lavender Lane.

"Good morning, Jane! Shall I prepare your usual delight?" Mrs. Dalloway's voice cut through the hum of the café, harmoniously blending cheer and intrigue. It wrapped around Jane like a warm, familiar embrace. The twinkle in her eye hinted at hidden depths beneath her genial facade, a spark of curiosity that matched Jane's own.

With a smile that reached her eyes, Jane replied, her tone light yet tinged with an undercurrent of anticipation, "You never miss, Mrs. D. Along with my coffee, is there perhaps any morsel of gossip to savor this morning?" Her eyes sparkled with a blend of jest and genuine interest, a testament to the bond formed over countless mornings shared in this very spot.

Lowering her voice to a conspiratorial whisper, Mrs. Dalloway leaned in, her movements deliberate, ensuring their conversation remained a cocooned secret amidst the café's gentle buzz. "You might find this particularly enthralling," she began, her eyes scanning the room before locking onto Jane's with an intensity that belied her usual jovial demeanor. "Have you perused today's newspaper? Another incident, mirroring the prior ones. It's the sole topic on everyone's lips."

Intrigued and slightly unnerved, Jane accepted the newspaper. Her hands brushed against the parchment with a mix of hesitation and curiosity. Her gaze quickly found the headline that screamed of a darkness encroaching upon their idyllic world: "Third Mosaic Murder Rattles Lavender Lane." The words seemed to leap off the page, each letter imbued with a sense of urgency and dread. A murmur escaped her, a mixture of disbelief and morbid fascination, "Another life taken, styled after ancient mosaics? How bizarre... and chillingly fascinating."

The air between them grew heavy with unspoken thoughts. The cozy ambiance of the café was momentarily overshadowed by the grim reality of the headline. Jane's mind raced, piecing together the implications of such crimes in a place as tranquil as Lavender Lane. The juxtaposition of her passion for ancient mosaics with the sinister mimicry of their beauty in acts of violence sent a shiver down her spine. She looked up from the paper, her eyes searching Mrs. Dalloway's for answers, for reassurance that the world they knew hadn't irrevocably changed.

Through expanded descriptions and atmospheric details, this passage immerses the reader deeper into the emotional and psychological world of the characters. By focusing on their actions, expressions, and the setting's reaction to the unfolding drama, it heightens the tension and intrigue, painting a vivid picture of a community on the verge of unraveling mysteries.

As Jane sipped her coffee, her mind swirled in a tempest of thoughts, mingling with the steam rising from her cup. Each sip drew her further into contemplation, as the rich, bold flavors of the brew mirrored the complexity of emotions she grappled with. Her life's work, dedicated to uncovering the stories and beauty enshrined in ancient mosaics, now found itself entangled in a narrative darker than any she had encountered in her studies. The idea that someone could pervert this art, transforming it into a tableau of death, struck her as a profound blasphemy against the craft she revered and as a riddle that persistently tugged at the edges of her mind.

"Do the authorities have any leads?" she asked, her voice a blend of hope and skepticism, as if searching for a lifeline amid uncertainty.

Mrs. Dalloway shook her head, her movements heavy with disappointment. The lines around her eyes deepened, silently testifying to her concern for the community and the seriousness of the situation. "They're at a standstill," she admitted, her voice conveying the helplessness that seemed to grip Lavender Lane. "Someone with your expertise might see what they cannot. Why not take a look, Jane? You might uncover something overlooked."

In that moment, a spark of resolve ignited within Jane, dissipating the mist of doubt clouding her determination. She placed her cup down with a decisiveness that reverberated through the café's walls, the clink of ceramic serving as a call to action. Standing up, she embodied newfound determination and her thoughts aligned with the precision of tesserae in the mosaics she loved. "Perhaps I will, Mrs. D.," she affirmed, her voice steady and infused with purpose. "If there's a dialogue in the language of mosaics, then it's one I must engage in."

This determination portrayed her not only as a scholar of ancient art but also as a seeker of truth, ready to venture beyond the confines of her academic pursuits into the shadows that lurked on the outskirts of her beloved Lavender Lane. The resolve in her eyes mirrored the resolve in her heart—a commitment to unravel not only this macabre mystery, but also to restore the sanctity of the art form that had been the passion of her life.

Through this expanded section, the emotional landscape of Jane is richly detailed, offering a window into her internal conflict and determination. The setting of the café serves as a backdrop to this pivotal moment, transforming from a place of refuge to a launchpad for Jane's journey into the unknown. The dialogue and descriptions intertwine to deepen the atmosphere, highlighting the transition from contemplation to action.

Exiting the café, Jane was greeted by a transformed world. The daylight, now at its zenith, cast long, dramatic shadows across Lavender Lane. The familiar cobblestones and ivy-clad facades became a scene simultaneously known and eerily foreign. Amidst this play of light and darkness, Jane's determination shone brightest, a beacon of resolve in a suddenly ambiguous world. She paused, taking in the altered visage of Lavender Lane, aware that not just the physical landscape had shifted, but the very fabric of her reality.

Her heartbeat with excitement tempered by trepidation, a symphony resonating with the pulsing life of the lane itself. "Stepping into the daylight, a whirlwind of excitement and trepidation engulfed me," Jane confessed. Her voice was a soft murmur against the backdrop of the bustling street, her words painting a vivid picture of her inner turmoil. "Unbeknownst to me, the path ahead was strewn with danger, deceit, and the unforeseen. But then again, what is life without its mysteries?" This rhetorical musing was not only a reflection of her thoughts, but also a challenge to herself, a reminder that the essence of life is found in navigating its uncertainties.

With each step, the weight of Jane's journey grew more palpable, the shadows on Lavender Lane transforming into silent spectators of her quest. The challenge before her was as thrilling as it was daunting, a labyrinthine puzzle that required not just her intellect and expertise, but also all the cunning, resilience, and perhaps, a dash of humor she could muster. The air around her crackled with anticipation, the lane itself holding its breath as she embarked on this precarious adventure.

Jane stood as a solitary figure against the contrasting light and shadow of Lavender Lane. The promise of danger, the allure of the unknown, and the magnetic pull of Jane's courage beckoned them forward, eager to follow her into the intricate and shadowy labyrinth that lay ahead. This wasn't just the start of a mystery; it was an invitation to join Jane on a journey that promised to traverse the very heart of what it means to seek, to find, and perhaps, to understand the enigma of Lavender Lane.

Alliance in Shadows: Forging a Path to Truth

THE LAVENDER LANE POLICE Department, with its imposing facade and steadfast structure, stood as a silent guardian over the town, embodying the collective resolve and unyielding spirit of the community it served. Its walls, weathered yet resolute, bore witness to the countless stories of hope, despair, triumph, and tragedy that unfolded within and beyond its precincts. As Jane approached, the weight of her mission pressed upon her, yet her stride remained unwavering, each step a testament to her resolve. Crossing the threshold, the atmosphere palpably shifted; her determination sliced through the air, leaving a trail of silent ripples in her wake.

The precinct buzzed with activity, a hive of urgency and purpose. Radios crackled, dispatch calls weaving a complex tapestry of sound throughout the room. The low drone of conversations, punctuated by bursts of activity, created a tension that was almost tangible. Amidst this cacophony, Jane stood as a beacon of calm determination, a stark contrast to the puzzled looks on the faces of the town's lawkeepers, unaccustomed to seeing a civilian amidst their chaotic daily endeavors.

Jane's internal voice grew stronger, a steady flame in the midst of chaos. "Who would have guessed that my fascination with relics of the past would lead me to the heart of modern-day investigations?" she mused, her thoughts a blend of wonder and resolve. "Yet, here I am, entangled in the mystery of the Mosaic Murders, as if destiny itself has woven it into the fabric of my life." This reflection, poised between awe and acceptance, underscored the surreal juxtaposition of her passion for ancient mosaics with the grim reality of the investigation that now consumed her attention.

As Jane awaited an audience with the lead detective, the precinct's rhythm of urgency and anticipation engulfed her, each tick of the clock marking the passage of time in a space where time often seemed both critical and elastic. Within this bubble of heightened reality, a familiar voice broke through her reverie, cutting through the layers of noise and activity with the precision of a well-tuned instrument. The voice, imbued with a warmth that seemed out of place in the sterile environment of the police department, offered a lifeline of normalcy amidst the storm. This sudden intrusion of familiarity into an otherwise foreign environment startled Jane, briefly grounding her in the midst of chaos. The juxtaposition of the buzzing energy of the police station and the comforting sound of a familiar voice highlighted the intricacies of Jane's journey. She had to navigate the murky waters of the Mosaic Murders investigation, carefully balancing her personal and professional life, as well as the past and the present.

As Jane stood amidst the bustling atmosphere of the police department, a voice broke through the noise with its unmistakable vibrancy and infectious enthusiasm. "Jane! I've heard that you're delving headfirst into this puzzle. You do know that you're not alone, right?" Lucy's voice was like a ray of sunshine piercing through the cloudy sky of Jane's thoughts, reminding her of the world outside the mystery that consumed her.

Turning toward her lifelong confidante, Jane's expression softened, and a genuine smile appeared, crinkling the corners of her eyes. There stood Lucy, amidst the chaotic procedures and stern faces of law enforcement, embodying unwavering friendship and support. "Lucy, your timing couldn't be better," Jane admitted with a sense of relief and gratitude. "I really need the company of a friend." Her words were simple yet profound, acknowledging the comfort and strength found in companionship, especially during times of uncertainty.

Lucy, ever the supportive pillar, responded playfully, a hint of mischief shining in her eyes, "And a friend you have. I've also brought reinforcements." Her voice conveyed a carefully devised plan, a testament to her commitment to stand by Jane and actively assist her in uncovering the heart of the mystery.

As Lucy spoke, a figure emerged from her side—Alex. Though new to Lavender Lane, his expertise in forensic analysis was evident. His entrance felt more like a revelation than an introduction, emanating a commanding yet unassuming presence. With sharp eyes that seemed to miss nothing, Alex surveyed the room with an analytical precision that spoke volumes. It was the gaze of one who had delved beneath the surface, deciphering the stories told in the absence of witnesses, attuned to the silent language of crime scenes.

Observing Alex's meticulous scrutiny of his surroundings, Jane felt a surge of hope. Here was someone whose expertise could illuminate the darkest corners of the case, a potential ally in her quest for truth. Alex's calm and collected demeanor stood in stark contrast to the frantic activity around them, hinting at a wealth of experience and a knack for observation that could prove invaluable. The introduction of Alex by Lucy not only strengthened Jane's determination but also expanded the scope of the narrative, introducing new dynamics and possibilities. The formation of an alliance within the police department, under the watchful eyes of Lavender Lane's finest, hinted at the convergence of past and present, intuition and evidence, in the unraveling of the mystery. This moment, brimming with potential and promise, marked a turning point in Jane's journey, weaving together the threads of friendship, expertise, and determination into a collective endeavor. "Jane, I presume?" The voice was unfamiliar but carried an air of confidence and curiosity. Lucy's introductions had always been filled with excitement, but this one felt different. Alex stood before her, representing both the unknown and the possibility of something greater. "Lucy has spoken highly of you, particularly regarding your expertise in ancient mosaics. I'm Alex. I believe I can contribute to this puzzle," he said, extending his hand in greeting.

Jane accepted the handshake, feeling the firm grip that reflected Alex's determination and the potential for a partnership that could bridge the gap between ancient art and modern crime. It was a handshake that symbolized more than just an introduction; it marked the beginning of a formidable alliance, an unspoken agreement to combine their separate realms of knowledge for a common goal.

The moment Jane had been anticipating broke through the anticipation like a guiding light. The detective, a figure of authority and experience, signaled to her from across the room. Introductions were quickly made, with Jane taking the lead, her voice calm and assured as she advocated for Lucy and Alex's involvement. There was a tangible pause from the detective, a moment heavy with skepticism and the weight of responsibility. His eyes, hardened by years of service, scrutinized the trio as if trying to assess their potential based on their determination alone.

"Fine, you're all in. But we follow the rules here. Understand?" he stated firmly, leaving no room for doubt. His gaze lingered on each of them, silently challenging them to prove their worth, yet underscored by a flicker of curiosity about their unique combination of skills.

"Understood, crystal clear. Let's get started," Jane affirmed, her voice filled with a confidence that seemed to envelop the space between them. Her response not only acknowledged the conditions laid out but also declared her readiness, a testament to her unwavering determination to delve into the heart of the mystery. The atmosphere in the room subtly shifted with this exchange, charged with a new sense of purpose and the beginning of a collaboration that defied conventional boundaries.

The detective's acknowledgement of their involvement marked a critical turning point, recognizing both the complexity of the case and the value of unconventional perspectives in the pursuit of truth.

As Jane, Lucy, and Alex prepared to dive into the investigation, they stood at the threshold of an endeavor that promised to challenge their skills, their understanding of the past, and their resolve to unearth the truth. The detective's cautionary words lingered in the air, reminding them of the structured path they needed to navigate within the realms of law and order. Yet beneath this directive, there was an undercurrent of anticipation. They shared an understanding that their journey together was about to unfold into depths unknown, guided by the light of their collective determination.

Convening around a table that buckled under the weight of the investigation's chaotic tapestry, crime scene photographs sprawled like a macabre mosaic amidst a sea of scattered notes and documents. The air was thick with concentration, the only sound the rustle of paper and the occasional clink of a coffee cup being set down too hastily.

Jane, with a historian's reverence for the past, elucidated the historical significance of the mosaics in question. Her hands moved with grace, tracing the patterns in the photographs, her voice bridging the ancient world with the present mystery. Alex, with a forensic eye, contributed insights that many would overlook. His observations were clinical yet imbued with a palpable respect for the gravity of his task.

Lucy, ever the linchpin of their dynamic trio, played the crucial role of intermediary. Her intuition acted as the loom upon which the disparate strands of their theories were woven into a coherent narrative. Her pointed questions often prompted deeper analysis, and her insights bridged gaps in logic and reasoning with ease, despite the complexity of the task at hand.

Pointing to a specific photograph, Alex's voice cut through the room's focused silence. "Notice the arrangement of these fragments. It's intentional, a deliberate choice. It's as though the killer is using the art to send a message." His finger hovered over the image, tracing the deliberate placement of the pieces, a silent testament to the meticulous planning of the perpetrator.

"And the message is...?" Lucy pondered aloud, her question hanging in the air like a challenge. Her eyes flicked between Jane and Alex, seeking in their faces the spark of revelation. "That's exactly what we're here to decipher," declared Jane with a resolute tone, her voice filling the room with determination. Her gaze remained strong, and her posture reflected her unwavering resolve. In this moment, the room, filled with evidence of human cruelty, seemed to fade away, leaving only the clarity of their purpose.

A glimmer of hope began to emerge in the darkness that surrounded them. This hope was not born out of naivety, but rather from the strength that came from their unity – Lucy's unwavering support, Alex's expertise in forensics, and Jane's deep understanding of the art that lay at the center of the mystery. Together, they stood on the precipice of unraveling a tangled web that intertwined ancient beauty with modern-day tragedy. With each stitch painstakingly unraveled, they knew that the path ahead was filled with uncertainty. Yet, in this moment of solidarity, the challenge felt not only manageable but conquerable. The journey into the heart of darkness was no longer a solitary pursuit but rather a shared quest for truth, with each member of the trio bringing their own unique light to dispel the shadows.

Echoes Through Time: The Clues Within

IN THE EMBRACE OF THE Lavender Lane Historical Museum, Jane and Alex found themselves immersed in a realm where history whispered secrets from the past. Bathed in soft, ethereal light, the room transformed each mosaic on its walls into a frozen narrative. These vibrant pieces, brimming with untold stories, echoed the macabre tableau of recent crimes, casting an ominous light on their beauty.

Jane's voice, barely more than a whisper in the dimness, carried a mixture of awe and urgency. "Notice here—these three red tiles," she delicately gestured towards a section of the mosaic, her fingers hovering but never touching. "They deviate from the original design. It's as though the murderer is weaving his own narrative into the ancient stories, leaving breadcrumbs for us to follow." Her eyes, alight with the thrill of discovery and the weight of their grim context, scanned the mosaic for further clues, her mind racing to connect the dots.

Alex, whose expertise in forensics often found order in chaos, leaned in closer, captivated by the anomaly Jane had highlighted. The comparison between the ancient artwork and the digital images of the crime scenes displayed on their tablet sparked a silent dialogue of parallels and patterns. "You're onto something," Alex murmured with a blend of admiration and resolve. "These alterations... they're more than just defacement; they're a map. A sinister guide to his next act." Their fingers swiped through the images on the tablet, tracing the invisible lines that connected past atrocities to potential future ones. "He's been steps ahead, cloaked in the shadows of history, using our heritage as his playground."

The weighty realization hung between them. The discovery of their quarry's method—this morbid intertwining of ancient art and modern-day murder—gave momentum to their quest. The air in the museum, usually still and laden with the dust of ages, now buzzed with urgent energy. Each mosaic piece, each fragment of history, transformed from a passive relic into an active clue in the unraveling of a mystery that straddled the boundary between past and present. This moment of clarity in the museum's dimly lit room was a turning point in their investigation. Surrounded by the silent witnesses of history, Jane and Alex were not mere observers but active participants in a narrative that continued to unfold.

Each discovery they made brought them closer to uncovering a villain who is using the blood of innocents as ink. As Jane and Alex delved deeper into their investigation, the shadows around them seemed to retreat slightly, as if their determination had begun to pierce the darkness that cloaked their path. "We must inform the authorities," Jane declared, her voice cutting through the heavy air of revelation. The gravity of the moment amplified her words, each syllable emphasizing the determination that shone in her eyes. "However, we must fully decipher this pattern before we proceed. There is no room for error." Her resolute stance in the dimly lit museum underscored the seriousness of their discovery. It was not just a declaration of intent, but a reminder of the meticulous care they must exercise as they unravel the clues before them.

Their investigation, which had initially been a journey through the shadows and whispers of the past, deepened into a symphony of shared knowledge and insight. Jane, with her profound understanding of ancient art, breathed life into the stories concealed within the mosaics. Each fragment was a piece of a larger narrative. Alex, with his eagle-eye for detail, brought forensic precision to their analysis. His expertise in deciphering the unseen marks of the present crime scene seamlessly merged with Jane's interpretations of the past.

Alex's finger paused on another mosaic, captivated by an anomaly that spoke volumes to those who could listen. "And here, look—this added tile bears a symbol from the Celtic calendar." His voice trembled with revelation, underscoring the significance of his find. Each puzzle piece they uncovered not only revealed their adversary's mindset but also wove a tapestry of intention spanning time and space. "Our adversary is not just marking locations; they are also delineating specific times."

Absorbing the implications of Alex's discovery, Jane was overcome by a mix of emotions. Struck by the ingenuity of their foe, she reluctantly felt a moment of admiration. "A timeline interwoven with antiquity..." she murmured, the concept unfurling within her mind like an ancient scroll. "Only someone as fascinated with the past as I am—or perhaps even more so—could conceive of such a complex scheme." Voicing her thoughts in the silence of the museum, Jane not only acknowledged the depth of their adversary but also recognized the shared ground upon which they stood, despite being on opposite sides of a vast chasm separating creator from destroyer.

The realization that Jane and her team were not only pursuing a shadow but also a brilliant mind intertwined with the corridors of history added a layer of complexity to their mission. It was a battle of wits set against the backdrop of time, a challenge that required not only expertise but also empathy in order to understand and anticipate the moves of their opponent - someone who, in many ways, reflected the darkness within their own souls. Their conversation, though brief, carried a heavy weight of acknowledgment for the intricate challenge they faced. However, amidst the gravity of their task, a sliver of humor managed to find its way through, momentarily lightening the atmosphere.

Half-jokingly, Jane mused with a playful undertone in her voice, "Let's hope he's not trying to give us a crash course in historical lore before we catch up to him." Her eyes twinkled in the dim light, reflecting the absurdity and depth of their quest.

Alex, momentarily softening his sharp forensic gaze with a smirk, agreed, "Indeed. I wasn't anticipating an exploration of ancient cultures being part of our agenda this week." His dry-witted comment lingered in the space between them, providing a brief respite from the pressing urgency of their investigation.

Having meticulously documented their discoveries, Jane and Alex emerged from the museum into the crisp clarity of the night. The outside air provided a stark contrast to the musty, time-saturated atmosphere they had left behind. The building, housing a treasure trove of history, faded into the darkness behind them like a silent sentinel guarding tales of ages past. However, the essence of their findings persisted as a beacon of hope in unraveling the mystery, an invisible thread connecting them to the heart of their investigation.

Jane gazed up at the night sky, where stars twinkled like distant lanterns guiding travelers through the ages. Reflecting, she whispered, "Under the watchful gaze of the stars, it felt as though the spirits of those ancient artisans were guiding our steps." Her thoughts reached out to the vastness above, finding solace in the notion that they were not alone in their quest. "Piece by piece, they are leading us through the labyrinth of their legacy, unveiling the truth hidden within their artistry.

"This moment, shared under the cover of the night, bridged the divide between the past and the present, between the concrete and the intangible. The bond Jane experienced with the skilled craftsmen of antiquity, whose creations they had diligently studied, appeared to infuse their undertaking with a more profound significance. It was almost as if the murmurs of history were directing them, proffering tacit hints in the interplay of darkness and illumination, spurring them onward through the maze of their inquiry toward the enigmatic truth concealed within layers of time and artistic prowess.

The Market's Whisper: Tracing the Echoes of Vengeance

IN THE HEART OF LAVENDER Lane, where a mysterious atmosphere had quietly settled over the town, the market flourished. It was a lively tapestry of life and color, pulsing with its own energy. Jane and Alex, acutely aware of the weight of their recent discoveries, made their way through the bustling crowd. Their seriousness contrasted starkly with the light-hearted banter and bartering around them. The market showcased a kaleidoscope of colors, from the vibrant shades of fresh produce to the deep, earthy tones of artisan crafts. These colors seemed to dance in the sunlight, almost tauntingly reminding them of the world's persistence despite the shadows lurking at its edges.

The cacophony of voices, a symphony of local dialects, laughter, and occasional negotiations, enveloped Jane and Alex. It weaved around them, creating a complex melody of life itself. Yet, amidst this vibrant chaos, their mission weighed heavily on them, each step forward a deliberate stride towards comprehension.

Jane silently reflected on the complexity of their journey as her thoughts flowed amid the external commotion. "Each step forward seemed to draw the past closer, casting long shadows that intertwined with the present in ways that felt almost destined." Her gaze, often captivated by the flutter of fabric or the glimmer of metalwork, saw beyond the market's facade. She sought the threads that connected the current moment to the tapestry of history they were unraveling.

Their destination within the market was a stall unlike any other, a quiet sanctuary of history amidst the clamor of modern life. The stall was adorned with fabrics that whispered tales of foreign lands with every fold and crease. Pottery bearing the marks of centuries, with each crack and chip testifying to its journey through time, shared the space. Jewelry glimmered not only with the shine of precious metals but also with the promise of untold stories. This alcove awaited them, inviting those passing by to peer into the past. The vendor, a figure as timeless as the artifacts he guarded, observed the world from under the shadow of his stall. His eyes carried a depth of knowledge and an understanding of the world that was as ancient as the items in his possession. When his gaze fell on Jane and Alex, it held both wisdom and a recognition of their purpose. In his presence, the market's fervor seemed to soften, providing a moment of solace and reflection for the two investigators as they approached. This encounter, set against the bustling market of Lavender Lane, was not just a meeting of individuals, but also a convergence of the past and present. It was a moment where the search for truth found its way to the doorsteps of history. Jane and Alex, standing before the sentinel of the past, were reminded that every piece of history held a story waiting to be told and a clue waiting to be discovered. As they continued their quest through the woven narratives of Lavender Lane, they were captivated by the mysteries that unfolded before them.

"May I assist you in your search? Or is it that a search has claimed you?" The vendor's deep and resonant voice seemed to weave through the air, enveloping the space in an air of ancient mystery. His piercing gaze seemed to penetrate beyond their external appearances, delving into the depths of their intentions. There was an undeniable wisdom in his eyes, a depth that had been acquired through years, or perhaps even centuries, of silent observation. It felt as if he could see through their façades and into the very heart of their quest.

With a knowing smile that hinted at the depth of her own journey, Jane responded, "We're drawn to your mosaics, particularly those that tell tales of extraordinary events." Her words were carefully selected, delicately skirting the weight of their investigation, yet imbued with a sincerity that conveyed her genuine intrigue and her hope that this encounter might shed light on their path.

The vendor's scrutiny seemed to intensify for a moment, his eyes narrowing as he tried to decipher the layers of meaning behind her words. Then, with a nod that acknowledged the gravity of their quest, he turned his attention to the cache of treasures he safeguarded. With deliberate movements, he delved beneath the draped fabrics and ancient artifacts, searching for a piece that had lain dormant, awaiting its moment of revelation.

Retrieving a fragment that hummed with an ominous energy, he carefully placed it before them. The mosaic shard depicted a scene that eerily mirrored the crimes they were investigating. Its vibrant colors were overshadowed by the darkness of its implications. "This shard has awaited its rightful guardian," he murmured in a voice that blended warning and wisdom, as if he were entrusting them with a sacred responsibility. "It whispers of betrayal, of a vengeance that spans the chasm of time." The air thickened with the weight of his words, and the ambient noise of the market faded into a distant murmur. The shard, with its haunting depiction, seemed to pulse with a life of its own. It silently bore witness to the atrocities reflected in his design. Jane and Alex, drawn into the gravity of the moment, could feel the resonance of the piece—an undeniable connection to the mystery they were determined to unravel. This encounter, observed by the vendor, went beyond a simple exchange. It symbolized a passing of knowledge, as the past entrusted its secrets to those willing to explore its depths. The shard, a key to unraveling a tale of revenge and betrayal, now rested in their hands. It acted as a guide, leading them deeper into the shadows of history and closer to the truth.

Alex examined the mosaic shard with the keen eye of a seasoned detective. His focused gaze revealed the hidden implications within the ancient artwork. "This may reveal the next chapter of our dark story,"

Alex pondered aloud. His voice conveyed both certainty and the weight of his discovery. "We must uncover the saga it belongs to." Each word carried the determination to delve deeper into the mystery, recognizing the shard as an illuminating force in his investigation.

As he delved into the lore surrounding the mosaic, fragments of history and whispers of the past began to form a narrative. The tale, while ancient in origin, sent a shiver down his spine with its echoes in the present. It spoke of unrequited love and a vengeful quest, mirrored by the chilling tableau created by the murderer haunting Lavender Lane. The parallels between this long-forgotten saga and the crimes unfolding in his community were unmistakable. Each horrifying act committed by the murderer was a dark reflection of this age-old story.

Jane could hardly contain her excitement as the pieces of the puzzle fell into place. Her eyes sparkled with the thrill of discovery. "This is the linchpin, Alex! Our adversary isn't merely committing crimes. He is resurrecting these ancient dramas, using them as inspiration for his atrocities." Her voice, a mix of horror and awe, emphasized the twisted genius of their foe. He sought inspiration from history to craft his modern-day horrors, using the past as a blueprint for his macabre narrative. This revelation, uncovered amidst the market's ancient relics, transformed their investigation. Jane and Alex now understood that their adversary's motives were rooted in the replication of historical vengeance. It was an intimidating task, but this newfound insight provided a crucial key to understanding the mind behind the crimes. As they contemplated their next move, the weight of history was upon them. It served as a solemn reminder of the cyclical nature of human emotions and the lengths to which a scorned heart would go to seek revenge.

With the fragment carefully secured between them and their resolve now iron-clad, Jane and Alex departed from the bustling market, stepping back into the quieter thoroughfares of Lavender Lane. The lane's quaint charm, with its cobblestone paths and gently swaying flower baskets, stood in stark contrast to the urgency coursing through their veins. Although the fragment seemed silent and unassuming in their possession, it held great weight as a symbol of the arduous journey that lay ahead—an expedition promising to venture into the depths of darkness beyond their initial expectations.

As they distanced themselves from the vibrant market, Jane's mind became a whirlwind of thoughts and theories. "The puzzle pieces began aligning, revealing a picture that grew increasingly complex with each revelation," she reflected, her voice laced with awe for their discoveries and the heavy implications they carried. Her gaze fixated on the road ahead, where the interplay of light and shadows seemed to mimic the unfolding mystery enveloping them.

"The whispers of the past have erupted into a clamor," she continued, her words imbuing the journey ahead with a sense of foreboding and intrigue. "Demanding our attention, they guide us through a labyrinth where every turn reveals a new shadow." Her determined steps, in sync with Alex's, echoed the firmness in her words. The once familiar lanes and alleyways of Lavender Lane now brimmed with secrets, every breath of wind urging them to delve deeper into the enigma at its core.

The fragment, now a bridge connecting the past to the present, had transformed from a mere artifact into a guiding light, illuminating their path forward. As they moved away from the market's cacophony, the ensuing silence bore the weight of history's whispers—tales untold, secrets waiting to be unveiled. United in their quest, Jane and Alex keenly felt the gravity of their mission, aware that the journey ahead would challenge not only their intellect and determination but also their courage to confront the darkness concealed within Lavender Lane's historical tapestry.

Rekindling Light: The Strength of Unbroken Bonds

IN JANE'S ONCE VIBRANT living room, which was once filled with shared discoveries and late-night debates, a different story unfolded. The atmosphere now held a quiet tension, threatening to estrange the once close friends. The walls, adorned with books and artifacts, whispered tales of ancient times, providing evidence of a lifetime dedicated to unearthing the past. But under the soft glow of a solitary table lamp, these whispers faded into the background, overtaken by a more pressing narrative.

This room, typically a sanctuary of warmth and camaraderie, had become a battleground for a silent conflict between connection and isolation. Shadows danced across the floor, reflecting the growing schism between the two friends caught in the midst of an unspoken disagreement.

Jane's internal monologue gave voice to the scene, her thoughts swirling with the complexity of their situation. "Behind every mystery lies a personal story. Ours is marked by the strain of a friendship struggling with doubt." Her introspective reflection acknowledged the invisible chasm that had formed, a divide not formed by malice but by the devoted focus her investigation required.

The stillness, disguising the underlying worry and frustration, was broken by Lucy's voice. "Jane, your obsession has created walls between us. You're here physically, but emotionally distant." Her words, filled with a mix of emotions, aimed to bridge the widening gap. "I'm trying to support you, but it feels like you're in a different world." The earnestness and concern in her voice begged for understanding and reconnection.

This moment, illuminated by the soft glow of the table lamp, became a turning point for Jane and Lucy. It was not only a confrontation of differing perspectives but a test of their bond - a bond challenged by the demands of Jane's all-consuming investigation. The surrounding artifacts, silent witnesses to their unfolding drama, reminded them of the delicate balance between the pursuit of truth and the nurturing of human connections.

As Lucy's words lingered in the air, Jane was faced with a choice - continue her relentless pursuit of the investigation or prioritize the preservation of a friendship that had endured many trials. In this quiet room, where the past and present collided, the way forward remained uncertain, dependent on their ability to find common ground amidst the chaos of their shared journey. Jane exhaled, her breath a tangible release of the myriad unshared burdens that had taken residence within her. The air around her seemed to momentarily thicken with the weight of her confession. "Lucy, it's not a choice to keep you at arm's length. This case... it's a labyrinth with no clear exit. It's all-consuming." Her words, infused with a weariness that went beyond physical exhaustion, painted a vivid picture of the internal struggle she faced—a battle not just against the external mystery but against the isolation it bred.

Lucy, undeterred by the gravity of Jane's admission, leaned in, her resolve crystallizing in the intensity of her gaze. It was a look that spoke volumes, a testament to her unwavering spirit and the depth of their bond. "Open the gates, then. Let me step into the maze with you. Don't sideline me, especially not now." Her voice, firm yet imbued with an underlying warmth, sought to breach the walls that Jane had unwittingly erected. "We've navigated through mysteries, through less and more, but this silence... it's like losing you to the echoes of the past and the mind games of a murderer."

The silence that followed was a canvas for reflection, a moment suspended between the spoken words and unvoiced fears. Jane's response, when it came, was a whisper, laden with vulnerability and the unguarded truth of her fears. "I'm sorry, Lucy. It never occurred to me—I've been so engulfed in these ancient whispers, drowning in a sea of cryptic sorrow and violence." Her admission, a window into the turmoil that churned beneath her composed exterior, revealed the extent of her immersion in the case. "My fear... it's that this darkness might swallow you too." Jane's eyes, a mirror to her soul, echoed the depth of her concern—a fear not for herself but for Lucy, a testament to the protective instinct that had driven her to maintain distance.

In this exchange, the living room, with its walls that had borne witness to the evolution of their friendship, became a crucible for their relationship's resilience. The shadows cast by the solitary table lamp, the shelves brimming with silent tales of yore, all faded into the backdrop as the focus narrowed to the space between Jane and Lucy—a space charged with the tension of confrontation and the potential for reconciliation. It was a pivotal moment, one that would define the path forward, not just in their quest to unravel the mystery but in the very fabric of their friendship, challenged yet enduring.

In the profound silence that surrounded them, a silence that seemed heavy with years of unspoken thoughts, the room itself became a vessel for the pivotal moment in their friendship. Lucy reached across the small gap that had felt like an insurmountable distance just moments before. It was a simple gesture, but within the context of their strained silence, it bridged the vast sea of uncertainties and fears between them. The soft lamplight bathed Lucy's face in a gentle glow, accentuating the sincerity in her eyes. "Jane, no matter how dark the night becomes, I'm here for you. You don't have to face this storm alone. Let me be the light that guides you through the darkness. We've always been unbreakable together, haven't we?"

Lucy's genuine tone, coupled with the symbolic bridge of her outstretched hand, burst the bubble of isolation that Jane had unknowingly trapped herself in. A fragile yet genuine smile graced Jane's lips, as if Lucy's words had ignited a flame within the depths of her heart that had been shrouded in darkness. Tears welled in her eyes, uninvited yet cathartic, reflecting the lamplight and the depth of emotion that Lucy's unwavering support had stirred. "Yes, we have. And I am more grateful than words can express. Let's face this storm side by side."

This exchange, bathed in the soft glow of Jane's living room, surrounded by silent witnesses of books and artifacts, stood as a testament to the enduring strength of their bond. A reminder that even in the face of daunting challenges and the darkness they brought, true friendship had the power to carve pathways through the most treacherous of labyrinths. The room, once filled with silent tensions, transformed into a sanctuary of renewed connection and shared determination.

As Jane accepted Lucy's hand, it was more than a physical connection; it symbolized unity, a silent vow to navigate the impending tempest with the combined strength of their spirits. The shadows seemed to recede, pushed back by the emerging light of their rekindled alliance, ready to face whatever the night held, together and unbreakable.

Beneath the gentle glow of Jane's living room lamp, the fractures that had threatened the foundation of their friendship began to mend, tied seamlessly together by the profound promise of solidarity. The ominous shadow of the case continued to loom over them, a constant reminder of the challenges that lay ahead. Yet, in this moment of quiet understanding and reconnection, the reaffirmed bond between Jane and Lucy shone with a brightness that pierced through the encroaching darkness, illuminating a path forward that had once been obscured by doubt and isolation. The room, a silent witness to the tumult and triumphs of their journey, seemed to envelop them in its warmth. The shelves of books and artifacts stood like old friends, acting as guardians, quietly joining in the celebration of their reconciled spirits. The very air felt charged with the energy of their renewed commitment to each other and the daunting path they had chosen to tread together.

In Jane's reflective conclusion, a soft, introspective voice interrupted the comfortable silence that had settled between them. "The journey through that night," she began, her gaze fixed on the distance as though visualizing the path they had traversed, "highlighted the essence of true friendship—not just reveling in the light, but also braving the darkness together." Spoken with conviction, her words echoed around the room, symbolizing the depth of her realization. "With Lucy's unwavering support, the once daunting path ahead now shone with the prospect of shared courage."

This acknowledgment, brimming with gratitude and newfound determination, served as a beacon of hope amidst the uncertainty of their quest. The challenges that lay in wait, though formidable, appeared less intimidating under the light of their fortified bond. The once overwhelming darkness now appeared as a landscape they could navigate, guided by the strength of their unity and the shared light of their courage.

As they sat in the tranquil comfort of Jane's living room, the world outside continued its restless dance, unaware of the profound shift that had occurred within those walls. For Jane and Lucy, the night had transformed from a source of fear into a canvas of possibility. It was painted with the broad strokes of friendship and adorned with the vibrant colors of shared determination.

The Letter's Echo: Unraveling the Threads of Fate

IN THE SECLUSION OF her study, Jane found herself captivated by the wisdom that adorned the walls. Books, keepers of forgotten tales and secrets, stood in solemn rows, their spines a mosaic of time-worn hues. Soft amber light valiantly battled the encroaching shadows, casting a tender and hesitant glow that enveloped the room. Yet, it was not enough to banish the secrets whispered by the corners.

Her desk, a chaotic landscape where enlightenment and disarray intertwined, bore witness to her passionate pursuit. Notes, scattered like leaves after an autumn storm, held the weight of ancient lore. Each shadow cast by the solitary lamp above melded into the mysteries of history, creating a visual symphony of light and darkness that mirrored her quest.

Jane's voice, a single thread woven into the tapestry of silence, resonated throughout the space. "In our search for truth," she mused, her gaze lost among the chaos of her desk, "the most profound discoveries often lie within the depths we least expect—hidden within the recesses of our own souls." Her words, spoken into the stillness, echoed a truth that surpassed the physical search she was undertaking, hinting at the inner journey into unexplored territories of heart and mind.

The study, with its blend of shadow and light, chaos and order, became a tangible manifestation of Jane's internal landscape. It was in this intimate space that she confronted not only the enigmas of history but also the mysteries of her own existence. Each revelation brought her closer to understanding not only the puzzles she sought to unravel but also the transformation taking place within herself.

The tranquility of Jane's study, a realm where time seemed to hold its breath, was abruptly shattered by a knock on the door. This simple sound, so strikingly out of place in the hushed reverence of the room, signaled the unraveling of a carefully woven tapestry of the past. The door, standing as a threshold between worlds, swung open to reveal Alex framed in the doorway. Their silhouette emanated the urgency of their mission as they clutched an aged letter, its edges frayed and yellowed with time—a treasure pulsing with untold stories.

"Gently," Jane began, her attention snapping to Alex. The interruption was a jarring note in the symphony of her solitude. "Jane, there's something you need to see." Alex's voice was a careful blend of caution and curiosity, weaving through the amber light and casting ripples in the still air. They stepped into the room, extending the letter towards her as if offering a key to unlock the shadows that danced just beyond understanding. The energy in the room shifted, the shadows seeming to lean in, eager for the revelation. Jane's gaze was drawn to the letter, a tangible connection to a past that had breached the present. The air felt charged, suspended between the known and the yet-to-be-discovered.

This seemingly insignificant letter was imbued with mystery and portent. It was a whisper from the past, reaching across the chasm of time. In its wake, the silent artifacts hummed with anticipation. The room, witness to countless hours of research and revelation, now held its breath, waiting for a new phase in their investigation.

Alex's arrival, once an intrusion, now felt like a necessary catalyst. He bore truths that were poised to shift the very ground of their quest. The study, with its layers of history and thought, braced itself for the impact of the letter's contents. A secret kept hidden through the ages was ready to unveil its story to those brave enough to listen.

The moment the letter was placed in Jane's hands, it came alive. The essence of bygone days seemed meticulously inked into its fibers. The yellowed and fragile paper trembled slightly, a testament to the weight of history it carried. Jane's fingertips grazed the surface, reverently tracing the curves of the script. Each letter echoed a love once vibrant, now dimmed by time and silence.

The handwriting was unmistakably that of a former lover. This companion had once shared Jane's insatiable passion for antiquity, now estranged by misfortune and regret. They had been more than just partners; they had been fellow travelers on a journey through history. Their shared dreams and discoveries were once the foundation of an unbreakable bond. Jane's voice trembled as she struggled to find the words, "This... how? Why now?" Her whisper seemed to dissolve into the weighty atmosphere of the study. Her disbelief was palpable, as memories long kept at bay resurfaced behind the fortress of her emotions. The letter, with its ancient script and deep personal meaning, acted as a key, unlocking a floodgate of emotions she thought she had safely tucked away in her past.

Once a sanctuary for intellectual pursuits, the study now felt like a stage set for the drama of Jane's life. Shadows stretched ominously in the dim light, reaching out to expose the secrets she buried deep within. The artifacts surrounding her seemed like silent witnesses to the intricate web of human relationships, capable of bringing both immense joy and unbearable pain. As Jane held the letter, the outside world faded away. The distant sounds of life on Lavender Lane retreated, leaving her encapsulated in a timeless bubble where past and present clashed. The words on the page, although silent, spoke volumes. Each sentence acted as a thread pulling her back to moments of happiness, heartache, and irreversible transformation. This unexpected correspondence wasn't simply communication across time; it was a mirror reflecting the fragmented fragments of her own soul, demanding that she confront the truths she had long avoided.

With each line Jane read, the letter unraveled a tale not just of love, but of a partnership entangled with ambition. It chronicled a time when two souls, driven by a shared vision, danced on the edge of greatness.

Their dreams cast long shadows into the future. Yet, as often happens when ambition burns too fiercely, their light turned to ashes, leaving behind a shared devastation. The dreams that once united them crumbled, leaving a void filled with the echoes of what might have been.

The heartfelt words, written with a tremor of emotion, concluded with a cryptic admission of responsibility. They acknowledged faults and regrets, paths taken and abandoned. The letter hinted at a prophecy, an enigmatic suggestion that their paths may cross again, implying not an end, but a pause in their shared journey that had stretched on for years.

"What does it say? Can you tell us?" Alex's voice cut through the heavy air of the study, his mixture of concern and curiosity jolting Jane back to the present. He shattered the spell of introspection that had consumed her, pulling her away from the precipice of memories threatening to consume her whole. Jane lifted her gaze from the letter, her eyes filled with a mix of nostalgia, sorrow, and a flicker of something else - perhaps hope or simply an acknowledgment of how the letter had forever changed her reality. "It's...a message from the past," she began, her voice expressing both wonder and wistfulness. "It's an admission of mistakes made and the potential for our paths to cross again." As she held the paper tighter, it seemed as though she believed that by doing so, she could bridge the gap between her past self and who she had become.

Watching the emotions play out across Jane's face, Alex remained silent, providing her with the space she needed to navigate her inner turmoil. The study, bathed in amber light with encroaching shadows, held its breath, as if the very air was waiting for Jane to decide how much of her past she was willing to reveal. The letter was nothing more than a piece of paper, and yet it held so much power. It had become a catalyst, forcing Jane to confront the complexities of human relationships - how they can both cause immense pain and serve as a guiding light back to forgotten places. In this moment, Jane and Alex were not only brought together by their physical proximity but also by the unspoken understanding that certain journeys must be undertaken internally before they can be shared.

"It's from a part of my life that I thought was closed - a soul that was once inseparable from mine," Jane's voice wove through the silence of the study, each word adding another thread to the tapestry of grief and epiphany that now enveloped her. Her eyes, reflecting the storm of realizations and memories, remained fixed on the letter as if it were a bridge to a past she had long left behind.

Within her, a revelation unfolded - an overwhelming understanding that fused the personal anguish of a lost love with the macabre dance of the murders that had haunted her every waking moment. With each sentence she read and each line of aged handwriting she deciphered, Jane could feel the ground shifting beneath her feet. What was once believed to be a sinister homage to ancient art now unraveled itself as a dark retelling of her own history - a narrative intricately woven with threads of passion, betrayal, and an unsettled ending.

As Alex observed the transformation taking hold of Jane, he noticed the color drain from her face as the weight of realization settled upon her shoulders. The room, once a sanctuary for intellectual pursuits and solitary contemplation, now bore witness to the merging of past and present - personal heartache entwined with a far more ominous story than either of them could have anticipated. "The murders... they're not simply imitating historical patterns. They're reflecting... us. Our story," Jane managed to articulate, her revelation suspended between them, a specter that neither had anticipated. The very air seemed to thicken with the weight of her words, as the soft amber light now cast long shadows that danced across the walls, mirroring the dark intertwining of fate that Jane and her former lover had become entangled in.

This pivotal moment, charged with the rawness of uncovered truths and the sharp sting of personal revelation, marked a turning point. Jane, clutching the letter tightly in her hand as though drawing strength from its tangible connection to her past, stood at the precipice of a journey not only to apprehend a killer but also to confront the specters of a chapter she had believed firmly closed. The path ahead, once a quest for justice in the realm of academia and abstraction, had been transformed into a pilgrimage through the shadowed valleys of her own life—a journey to unearth the roots of a tale that had blossomed into something far more insidious than she had ever imagined.

"This revelation reshapes our pursuit," Jane declared, her voice no longer just a vessel for her shock but now infused with a newfound determination that seemed to solidify the air around her. "The perpetrator isn't merely echoing the artistry of the past; they are painting with the colors of my life, creating their malevolence on the canvas of my memories." Her words, resolute and laden with implication, reverberated within the room, echoing off the walls adorned with the silent witnesses of her accumulated knowledge and now, her personal saga.

As she stood up from her seat, her actions seemed to bear the full weight of the discovery, her resolve grounding her as she prepared to confront the converging paths of her past and the present enigma. Alex, witnessing this transformation, stood by her side, his presence a silent testament to the depth of his commitment. The exchange of glances between them carried an unspoken vow of allegiance; their eyes, reflecting a shared understanding that transcended words, acknowledged the altered nature of their endeavor. The mystery they were entwined in was no longer a remote puzzle to be solved, but an odyssey into the core of Jane's being—a narrative indivisibly linked to her own.

Jane's closing thoughts were a solemn reflection that seemed to reverberate in the room's stillness. She said, "With every piece that finds its place, the narrative sharpens, drawing not only into the light of truth but into the shadows of my own past." As her gaze drifted over the artifacts in her study, she found new meaning in their silent company. "This journey goes beyond the search for a murderer; it is an expedition into the very core of my existence." The solemnity in her voice emphasized her realization. The pursuit of justice had transformed into a deeper, more introspective journey, challenging her to confront and reconcile the fragmented pieces of her life. The room, once a refuge from the world's noise, now felt like the launching pad for a journey of unparalleled personal significance. The shadows cast by the solitary lamp stretched out, as if reaching towards the unknown, mirroring the path that lay ahead for Jane. This path, illuminated by the revelations of the night, promised not only the pursuit of a killer but also the exploration of the labyrinthine corridors of Jane's own memories and identity—a journey filled with the promise of discovery and the peril of confronting what lay hidden in the depths.

The Mosaic of Truth: Unveiling the Art of Deception

WITHIN THE GRANDEUR of the Lavender Lane Art Museum, an event unfolded that mirrored the opulence of its setting. The hall, adorned with relics of a bygone era and cutting-edge expressions of contemporary genius, thrummed with laughter and the clink of fine glassware. The air was perfumed with expensive cologne and the subtle aroma of gourmet delicacies, creating an atmosphere of cultivated elegance. However, beneath the veneer of festivity and cultural appreciation, an undercurrent of drama was poised to ripple through the gathered elite. Souls, dressed in their finest, mingled in blissful ignorance of the impending drama, their conversations a mix of trivialities and grandiose statements.

Jane, however, stood apart from the gaiety, a solitary figure amidst the sea of revelry. She dressed not to dazzle but to blend, her attire elegant yet understated, reflecting her purpose in being there. Her gaze was fixed, with hunter-like precision, on a figure who commanded the room not just with his prominence in the art world but also for the unknowing role he played in a narrative far darker than any creation within his galleries. Surrounded by admirers and sycophants, the man remained oblivious to the storm about to break over him—a storm brewing in the depths of Jane's determined pursuit.

Jane's inner voice, steady and introspective amid the chaos, reflected on the journey that led her to this moment. "The puzzle, once fragmented and obscure, has coalesced into a portrait stark in its implications, revealing a truth both unforeseen and hauntingly familiar." Her thoughts, a calm center amidst the whirlwind of emotions,

37

acknowledged the surreal convergence of her past and present. Each piece of the enigma, painstakingly unearthed from the shadows of history and the recesses of her memory, now fit together in a portrait that was revealing and damning.

As she prepared to confront the man at the nexus of her investigation, Jane was acutely aware of the dual nature of the setting. The museum, a repository of beauty and a testament to human creativity, was about to become the backdrop for the unveiling of a truth as ugly as it was necessary. This juxtaposition was not lost on her; the art that surrounded them, each piece a story of its own, stood as silent witnesses to the complexity of human nature, capable of creating both breathtaking beauty and devastating destruction.

The grandeur of the event, with its light-hearted facade, was a stark contrast to the gravity of Jane's mission. As the laughter and music swirled around her, Jane prepared herself for the impending confrontation, the culmination of a journey that had delved into the depths of human passion and folly. Tonight, the Lavender Lane Art Museum wasn't just a venue for cultural celebration; it was a stage where the final act of a long-unfolding drama was about to unfold, under the watchful eyes of the past and the tense anticipation of one determined woman.

With a poise that masked the turmoil within her, Jane moved through the crowd with purpose. The opulent hall, filled with Lavender Lane's elite, seemed to part for her as a silent acknowledgement of her determination. Her approach was deliberate, carrying with it the weight of inevitability, capturing the attention of onlookers who sensed, perhaps subconsciously, a shift in the evening's narrative.

Adrian Bellefonte, a charismatic figure amidst the glittering assemblage, stood surrounded by admirers. His charm was as radiant as the art that adorned the museum's walls. However, as Jane emerged from the crowd, a shadow crossed his face, momentarily interrupting his otherwise flawless demeanor. The slight unease that flickered behind his practiced smile was the only crack in the facade he presented to the world.

"Jane, what brings you here tonight?" Adrian managed, his voice smooth as silk, attempting to disguise his astonishment as casual curiosity. Though his words were delivered with the polished ease of a man accustomed to social maneuvering, they thinly veiled the tension that Jane's presence evoked.

The air between them was charged, a silent battleground where unspoken words and withheld truths wrestled for dominance. The backdrop of the event faded into irrelevance, leaving Jane and Adrian encapsulated in their own private bubble, where the stakes were both personal and profound.

Jane's response was measured, her voice steady amidst the chaos of the gala. "Adrian, we both know this is more than a social visit." Her unyielding gaze met Adrian's, a clear challenge to the layer of civility that lay between them.

The moment marked the convergence of past and present, a nexus where their shared history and the impending revelations of the night collided. Adrian, caught in the spotlight of Jane's scrutiny, found his usual composure tested by her intensity — a reminder that the evening's opulence could not shield him from the truths she carried. In the Lavender Lane Art Museum, Jane and Adrian stood poised for an unveiling that would expose the truth beneath their polished facades. The atmosphere was charged with anticipation as the gathering witnessed this long-awaited clash of wills, aware that each move and word would shape the narrative that had intertwined their lives.

Jane dispensed with pleasantries and confronted Adrian with surgical precision, determined to cut through the carefully constructed illusion he had created. "Adrian, spare me the charade. The twisted love story you've woven along Lavender Lane ends tonight," she declared, her voice carrying undeniable authority that hung in the air between them. Her quiet words echoed through the hall, perceptible only to the two of them amidst the revelry.

Adrian's demeanor visibly shifted upon her accusation. The affable mask he wore began to slip, revealing a hint of genuine unease. The practiced smile that endeared him to the art elite faded, replaced by a subtle, telling tightness at the corners of his mouth in response to Jane's weighty words. "Accusations require evidence, Ms. Doe," he retorted, maintaining his polished tone but overlaying it with a cold sharpness. "You tread on thin ice with mere supposition." Although his response carried defiance, it also betrayed a hint of defensiveness, revealing a crack in his armor brought on by Jane's directness.

The transformation in Adrian's posture mirrored the shift in their exchange. The space surrounding them, once animated by the gala's hum, seemed to shrink, becoming an intimate arena for their verbal duel. The ambient light, casting dramatic interplays of light and shadow across their faces, intensified the gravity of the moment against the opulent backdrop.

In this confrontation, the Lavender Lane Art Museum, with its cultural treasures and trappings, became a mere stage for the human drama unfolding before it. The stakes were laid bare, not in the language of art and aesthetics that Adrian so expertly wielded, but in the stark, unadorned truth that Jane brought to bear. Their dialogue, a dance of accusation and denial, went beyond a clash of wills; it manifested the underlying tensions that had simmered beneath the surface of their past interactions. Jane, armed with unwavering resolve, stood firm as Adrian attempted to deflect and diminish her. In this moment, the museum hall, a witness to countless unveilings, bore witness to one more: a revelation not of art, but of character. The true nature of the individuals behind their facades was laid bare for all to see.

But Jane, armed not only with conviction but also tangible evidence, remained unshaken in the face of Adrian's attempts to undermine her stance. Her resolve was evident in her posture and the clarity of her gaze. "This is no mere conjecture," she countered, her voice steady and filled with unwavering confidence. "The mosaics' narrative, your clandestine romance, the victims—it's a tapestry of desire, obsession, and deceit. And I hold the thread that unravels it." Her declaration, potent and unequivocal, left no room for doubt, painting a vivid picture of the intricate web spun around the unsuspecting victims.

The already tense confrontation reached its climax as Alex and Lucy, previously shadows at the edge of the unfolding drama, stepped forward. Their presence, solid and unwavering, physically manifested the support that had bolstered Jane's quest from the shadows. The approaching silhouette of law enforcement, barely recognizable at first, grew steadily, casting a long and ominous shadow over Adrian's final moments of freedom. The gala's opulent lighting dimmed, seemingly in anticipation, turning the festive atmosphere into a stark backdrop for the unfolding reckoning.

Adrian's resistance, once fortified by denial and bravado, crumbled under the weight of Jane's revelations. The fortress of secrets he had meticulously constructed over many years was breached by the relentless tide of truth unleashed by Jane. His previously rigid posture of defiance sagged, as if the air itself had thickened, pressing down upon his shoulders with the weight of his impending fate.

The hall, a witness to this dramatic denouement, seemed to hold its breath as the reality of the situation settled over the assembled guests. Whispers rippled through the crowd, a growing wave of realization and disbelief filling the air. The grandeur of the Lavender Lane Art Museum, once a mere backdrop for a high-society gala, had transformed into the stage for a moment of irrevocable change. It was not just a change in the life of Adrian Bellefonte, but in the lives of all who had been touched by the shadow of his actions. As law enforcement officers made their presence known, moving purposefully through the crowd, the finality of the moment became clear. Adrian, now diminished not only in his own eyes but also in the eyes of all who witnessed his fall, stood as a testament to the power of truth— a truth that Jane, with the support of her allies, had brought to light against all odds.

"How?" Adrian whispered, his question more of a realization of his situation. The sense of control and charisma that had defined him slipped away, leaving him exposed in the grand hall of the museum. Jane's response lacked triumph but carried a nuanced mix of sorrow for what had been lost and a clear understanding of the path that had led them to this moment. "You chose a medium too close to my heart, Adrian," she said, her voice heavy yet freeing. Her eyes, reflecting the depth of her journey, met his with unwavering steadiness. "The echoes of history, of personal loss—they spoke a language of betrayal and redemption."

Soft yet unwavering, Jane's words filled the space between them, imbuing the air with a profound sense of truth and consequence. "You underestimated the resonance of the past," she concluded, exposing the heart of Adrian's mistake. It wasn't just the act of blending deceit into historical art that led to his downfall; it was his failure to comprehend Jane's connection to that history and her innate ability to unravel its whispers of betrayal and redemption.

The museum, with its interplay of shadows and light on statues and paintings, bore witness to this moment of revelation. The assembled crowd, once a mere backdrop, now observed in hushed anticipation, the gravity of Jane's words and the realization of Adrian's fall from grace hanging heavy in the air.

Faced with the depth of Jane's insight, Adrian felt the walls he had constructed— the lies, the manipulations— crumble under the weight of her understanding. The art that had served as his refuge, a tool for his schemes, now became the instrument of his exposure, interpreted by the one person he had underestimated.

In this charged atmosphere, the unfolding drama transcended personal vendettas and delved into universal truths about the power of the past to shape, torment, and ultimately reveal. Jane's confrontation with Adrian, against a backdrop of cultural legacy and personal tragedy, highlighted a narrative far more intricate and profound than the sum of its parts. It served as a testament to the indomitable strength of the human spirit in the face of deceit and loss.

As Adrian was escorted away, his silhouette shrinking against the grandeur of the Lavender Lane Art Museum, the atmosphere palpably shifted. The vibrant energy that had animated the backdrop of the art world dimmed, as if the very essence of the evening's exuberance had been siphoned away, leaving behind a quieter, more contemplative space. Jane, Lucy, and Alex found themselves enveloped in this new atmosphere, standing amidst the remnants of the gala that had transformed before their eyes.

The three of them, bound by a journey that had tested their limits and revealed the depths of their bond, shared a moment of sober reflection. Their camaraderie, forged in the crucible of adversity, stood as a testament to their collective resilience. The trials they had endured, the truths they had uncovered, had not tarnished their connection; instead, it emerged unscathed, perhaps even strengthened by the challenges they had faced together.

In the wake of the upheaval, surrounded by the silent witnesses of art lining the walls, Jane's thoughts turned introspective. Though no words were spoken, her closing reflections resonated in the shared silence between them, a silent communion that spoke volumes. "The saga's conclusion reminded us," she reflected, "that the essence of the mosaic lies not solely in ancient relics but in the narratives we craft within our lives." In her mind's eye, she saw not just the physical mosaics they had studied but the metaphorical mosaic they had lived—an intricate tapestry woven from moments of joy and pain, success and failure.

"Each fragment, some resplendent, others fractured, yet all indelibly linked in the mosaic of human experience." Her silent musings underscored a profound lesson gleaned from their journey. The events that had unfolded, the revelations that had come to light, were but pieces of a larger puzzle, fragments of a greater narrative that spanned beyond the confines of their investigation.

As they stood together in the muted aftermath of the gala, the echoes of their ordeal weaving a subtle but indelible pattern into the fabric of their lives, they were reminded of the intricate beauty of human connection. The art around them, each piece a testament to the artist's vision and struggle, mirrored their own journey—one marked by complexity, by the intertwining of light and shadow, and ultimately, by the enduring strength found in unity.

In this moment, Jane, Lucy, and Alex were not just witnesses to the resolution of a mystery but participants in a shared story, their lives irrevocably intertwined in the mosaic of human experience, each bringing their unique color and texture to the collective masterpiece that was their friendship and their triumph.

Echoes of Triumph: Reflections in the Shadows of Art

IN THE SHADOWED RECESSES of the Lavender Lane Art Museum, away from the luminous gala and the eyes of the world, a final confrontation unfolded with a gravity that matched the historical and artistic gravitas surrounding them. The air was thick, charged with the anticipation of truths long obscured, now poised for revelation. Amidst relics that spoke of beauty and history, the setting was a poignant reminder of the stark contrast between creation and destruction, between the enduring legacy of art and the ephemeral nature of deceit.

Jane, Lucy, and Alex stood united, a bastion of resolve against the impending storm. Their collective strength, forged in the fires of adversity and the pursuit of justice, made them an immovable force. Across this divide, Adrian Bellefonte, once a master of manipulation ensnared in the intricate web of his own making, faced them. His posture, though defiant, bore the unmistakable signs of defeat—a once towering figure, now diminished by the weight of his impending unraveling.

Jane's voice, infused with a firmness that echoed off the ancient walls, cut through the thick silence that had settled in the room. "The end of the road, Adrian. The twisted narrative you've woven—of illicit passions, of lives taken, of art perverted—it all unravels here." Her words, clear and unwavering, resonated not just in the physical space but in the moral chasm that separated them from Adrian. Each syllable was a nail in the coffin of the facade Adrian had so carefully constructed, a declaration that the time for obfuscation was over.

The confrontation, set against the backdrop of timeless art, was a vivid tableau of the eternal struggle between light and shadow, truth and deception. The museum, with its hallowed halls bearing witness to the pinnacle of human creativity, now hosted a drama that was as human as the stories encapsulated within its walls. The irony of their surroundings—a place dedicated to the celebration of human achievement, now the stage for the exposure of human frailty—was not lost on those present.

As Jane concluded her indictment, the atmosphere seemed to shift, a tangible manifestation of the transfer in power from Adrian to those he had sought to manipulate. Lucy and Alex, standing by Jane, were silent pillars of support, their presence a reminder that while the path to truth is often a solitary journey, its burdens need not be carried alone. Adrian, for his part, stood as a figure both tragic and admonitory, a testament to the corrosive power of unchecked ambition and desire. The silence that followed Jane's declaration was a canvas for reflection, a moment suspended in time where the echoes of the past and the whisper of redemption hung in balance. In the dimly lit corner of the Lavender Lane Art Museum, amidst artifacts that bore witness to centuries of art and culture, a modern tragedy unfolded. It was a confrontation that, though rooted in the present, reflected a timeless aspect of the human condition.

Adrian, once the epitome of sophistication and charm, now stood with a sneer that distorted his features beyond recognition. The shadows of the museum seemed to gather around him, drawn to the darkness that emanated from within. "You claim victory, yet you fail to understand the essence of my work—a tribute to a passion so profound, it surpasses ordinary comprehension," he retorted, his voice dripping with bitterness. "Of all people, you should recognize the sacrifice made for art." His words, intended to defend himself, echoed hollowly in the grandeur of their surroundings, highlighting the stark contrast between his hollow defense and the beauty and humanity manifested in the art around them.

Lucy, her stance rigid with indignation, faced Adrian head-on. The tension in her body spoke volumes, a visible manifestation of her outrage. "What you call sacrifice, we call madness," she countered, her voice cutting through the air with sharp clarity. "Your 'art' serves as a cover for atrocity." Her words, resolute and unequivocal, reverberated through the museum halls, challenging the silence that had descended upon the confrontation.

The air crackled with the clash of their convictions, while the museum's artifacts and masterpieces stood as silent witnesses to the moral battlefield before them. The rich tapestries and ancient sculptures, embodiments of true artistic endeavor and sacrifice, seemed to mock Adrian's justification of his actions.

The museum, a sanctuary of human expression and creativity, felt almost suffocating under the weight of the moment. The dim lighting cast long shadows, intensifying the scene with dramatic effect, underscoring the gravity of Lucy's accusation and the delusion present in Adrian's defense. In this charged atmosphere, the dialogue between Lucy and Adrian transcended mere words—it became a clash of ideologies, a confrontation between the sanctity of artistic expression and its perverse distortion. Adrian, isolated in his misguided beliefs, confronted the united front of Jane, Lucy, and Alex, who stood as champions of the truth. Their resolve remained unbroken, undeterred by the darkness they sought to dispel. Alex, who usually exuded a contemplative calm, stepped forward with the very embodiment of composed rationale. His intense focus sliced through the tension in the air as he interjected, his voice cold and logical yet fueled by conviction, "And beyond the bounds of law. Your tapestry of deception is undone. It's time to face the music, Adrian." Each word, meticulously chosen, hammered another nail into Adrian's constructed reality, dismantling the facade he had so carefully created.

In response, Adrian reacted not with contrition, but with defiance. A hollow laugh, devoid of genuine mirth but weighed down by the crumbling facade, resonated from him. It was a chilling sound, its echoes bouncing off the museum's grand walls—a reminder of his refusal to grasp the gravity of his situation. "You think you've bested me?" he jeered, his voice simultaneously filled with scorn and a peculiar kind of triumph, as if he still saw himself as the maestro in this macabre symphony. "My legacy is etched in the annals of time, an indelible mark on the canvas of history."

Despite his grandiose words, Adrian's resolve wavered against the unwavering determination of Jane, Lucy, and Alex. The museum, adorned with statues and paintings, became the stage for this moment of reckoning—a striking contrast between Adrian's illusions of greatness and the tangible reality of justice about to be served.

Set against the backdrop of centuries of genuine artistry and human achievement, this final exchange highlighted the tragically absurd nature of Adrian's claims. His so-called "legacy," built on cruelty and deceit, was nothing more than a dark stain—a cautionary tale of how obsession can tarnish beauty and talent. The true legacy, as exemplified by the resolve and unity of those who stood against him, was one of courage—a relentless pursuit of truth and the preservation of human life over the misguided romanticization of suffering for art's sake. As Adrian's hollow laughter faded into the charged silence, Jane, Lucy, and Alex remained resolute—a beacon of light in the darkness that Adrian had sought to inflict. Their victory went beyond dismantling one man's delusional narrative; it reaffirmed the enduring power of truth, justice, and the indomitable human spirit. Jane's unwavering gaze locked onto Adrian with an intensity that seemed to penetrate through his defiant exterior. Her calm stance contradicted Adrian's faltering bravado, exuding the unshakable strength of her convictions. "But at what cost?" she replied, her voice resonating with both sorrow for the victims and a scathing critique of Adrian's rationalizations. "The lives you've shattered, the light you've extinguished—no work of art justifies such devastation." Her clear and potent words lingered in the air, underscoring the gravity of Adrian's crimes and the indefensible nature of his actions.

As the authorities silently but inexorably closed in, the tension in the room reached its peak. The soft click of handcuffs echoed like a gavel in the museum's hushed atmosphere, signaling the end of Adrian's freedom and the culmination of Jane's relentless pursuit of justice.

In that moment, Jane and Adrian exchanged a silent understanding that transcended words. It was a mutual recognition of the intellectual battle that lay at the heart of their confrontation, a clash of wits and wills that had now reached its inevitable conclusion. Adrian's once fiery eyes flickered with the realization of his defeat, while Jane's reflected a somber victory tinged with the high cost at which it had been achieved.

This silent acknowledgment, shared in the fleeting seconds before Adrian was taken away, was a complex tapestry woven with regret, understanding, and the irreversible consequences of their choices. It served as a poignant reminder that their personal struggle also embodied broader themes of justice, morality, and the delicate boundary between genius and madness.

The grandeur of the Lavender Lane Art Museum, with its priceless artifacts and solemn beauty, stood as a silent witness to this human drama, embodying the enduring power of art to inspire, provoke, and in this case, reveal the depths to which one could sink in its name. The legacy of this night, marked by the resolution of a harrowing tale of obsession and loss, would reverberate through the museum's halls long after the echoes of Adrian's footsteps had faded away.

With a semblance of grace that belied the weight of his defeat, Adrian conceded, his voice tinged with resignation and philosophical musings. "Perhaps you've cornered me, Jane, but consider this—the shadow of an artist, their essence, lives on, etching itself into the fabric of eternity, long after their flame has been extinguished." His farewell words left a lingering question in the air, challenging the concept of legacy and the indelible mark one leaves on the world, for better or for worse.

As they witnessed Adrian's form merging into the darkness of the night, the Lavender Lane Art Museum seemed to exhale a collective sigh, relieving the tension that had built up throughout the evening. The absence left by his departure was tangible, a silence that resonated through the halls, filled with centuries of artistic endeavors and human expression.

In the aftermath, Jane, Lucy, and Alex exchanged glances, their faces subtly illuminated by the museum's soft lighting. The mixture of emotions reflected in their eyes conveyed both a sense of relief from the immediate threat and a contemplation of the deeper implications of their ordeal. The victory they achieved was not without its shadows, reminding them of the dual nature of humanity—capable of both creation and destruction, of both beauty and devastation.

The impact of their experience lingered in the air, a silent testament to the journey they had embarked upon. It was not just the conclusion of a case, but also a reflection on how their actions and choices wove into the fabric of history. Adrian's final words reverberated not as a justification for his deeds, but as a contemplation on the lasting essence of creativity and its consequences.

As night reclaimed the museum, Jane, Lucy, and Alex stood united in the stillness, their bond strengthened by the trials they had faced. Although the immediate danger had passed, the echoes of their experience would persist, serving as a constant reminder of the complexities of art, justice, and the human heart. Ultimately, their ordeal became a testament to the enduring power of resilience, the triumph of light over darkness, and the unbreakable strength found in unity.

In the aftermath, as the echo of Adrian's departure faded into the vast, shadowed embrace of the Lavender Lane Art Museum, a contemplative atmosphere settled. Jane's silhouette, framed by the subtle glow of ancient artifacts, embodied a figure both triumphant and introspective. Her voice, when she spoke, carried the weight of their collective journey, evoking an attentive audience among the lurking shadows. "As Adrian's figure receded into the museum's embrace, the duality of our triumph became clear," he began, his words floating in the serene air. The museum, a silent witness to the unraveling of a man consumed by obsession, now stood as a testament to their unwavering resolve. "The mystery has been unraveled, the future secured, but it has come with an introspection of the darkest corners of our own capabilities." His gaze, lost in the dim corridors surrounding them, conveyed a profound struggle—a battle fought not only against Adrian's machinations but against the darker aspects of human nature they had been forced to confront. This journey was not just a pursuit of justice but also a reflection of the darkness that resides within the soul. Jane's profound and resonant contemplation captured the essence of their experience, a declaration that their triumph was tinged with the somber realization of the extremes of human nature—the heights of bravery and sacrifice, as well as the depths of cruelty and despair.

Standing alongside Jane, Lucy, and Alex shared in this moment of solemn realization. Illuminated by the scarce light, their expressions were a complex blend of relief, sorrow, and newfound wisdom. The museum, housing a vast collection that spanned the spectrum of human achievement and folly, echoed Jane's sentiments—a quiet reminder that art, like their journey, often mirrors the dualities of the human condition.

During this introspective pause, the trio stood not only as victors but also as philosophers, contemplating the lessons learned from the darkness they had confronted. The night, with its stars obscured by the city's glow, enveloped the museum in a hushed atmosphere that seemed to make room for their reflections.

Their triumph served as a beacon, a light that pierced the shadows of human depravity, yet it cast its own long shadows. In the stillness of the museum, amidst remnants of past civilizations and the echoes of their own ordeal, Jane, Lucy, and Alex were reminded that the journey through darkness is not only an outward path but also an inward voyage into the depths of the human spirit.

The Dawn of Revelation: Unfolding the Tapestry of the Past

IN THE SANCTUARY OF her study, where the soft, diffused light of dawn seeped through the windows, casting gentle hues across the room, Jane found herself surrounded by countless books. Each spine, each page, whispered tales of worlds beyond and the wisdom of ages—a testament to humanity's endeavor to know, to feel, and to understand. Here, in this haven of thought and memory, Jane encountered not a crossroads of paths, but a crossroads of time itself. The letter she held tenderly in her hands was more than paper and ink; it was a bridge across time, a missive from a bygone phase of her life that now, eerily, intertwined with the tumultuous narrative of the present.

With a voice tinged with reflective melancholy, a reflection of the tranquil space around her, Jane broke the stillness. "There comes a juncture in every tale that divides the journey into a 'before' and an 'after.' For me, that division was heralded by the discovery of this letter—an echo from a past I thought I had left behind." Her words hung in the air, mingling with the dancing light and dust motes, creating a moment that was both ethereal and profoundly grounded.

Her eyes, tracing the faded lines of the letter, not only saw the words but also felt the weight of the emotions they carried—love, hope, despair, and the ultimate surrender to fate. It was a window to a time when her heart had been unguarded and exultantly alive, now shadowed by the complexity of her current reality.

As the morning light grew stronger, illuminating the contours of her face and revealing the depth of her contemplation, Jane found herself adrift in the sea of her own narrative. This letter, a relic of her past, had become the catalyst for profound introspection, challenging her to reconcile the woman she had become with the girl she once was.

"The discovery of this letter," she continued, her voice a mere whisper now, as if in reverence to the dawn and the revelations it brought, "has not only unearthed buried memories but also illuminated the path I must now tread." In her study, surrounded by the embodiments of human thought and creativity, Jane confronted the dichotomy of her existence—the immutable past and the malleable present, both converging in the heart and soul of one who had loved, lost, and dared to love again.

In this moment of solitude, with the day signaling new beginnings and the letter connecting her to her past, Jane stood at the edge of comprehension, prepared to embrace what comes next with a heart fortified by previous hardships. The study, a haven that had seen her spirit grow and change, was illuminated by the gentle morning light, creating a space for this significant moment in her story—a story that involved both reflection on the past and hope for the future.

As Lucy entered the room, her presence cut through the heavy atmosphere of reminiscence like a refreshing breeze through a stifling room. The early sunlight seemed to follow her, dispelling shadows and adding a comforting sense of normalcy to the study's thoughtful and nostalgic ambiance. Her gaze, filled with empathy and curiosity, scanned the room before settling on Jane, who, lost in deep contemplation, appeared burdened with reflection.

"What are you holding, Jane?" Lucy's question broke the silence, her voice gentle, weaving through the room with a tenderness that revealed her concern. There was a tangible empathy in her approach, an understanding of the weight of the moment they were experiencing together.

Exhaling a weary sigh, filled with unspoken revelations, Jane turned to face Lucy, her expression a complex blend of acceptance and determination. "It's a letter from a chapter of my life that I thought had ended, Lucy," she replied, her voice heavy with acknowledgement and a hint of resurfaced memories. "It seems the mysteries we're unraveling are deeply connected to my own story, far more than I could have anticipated." Jane's words, charged with their implications, hung between them, acknowledging the interwoven nature of personal history and their current entanglement.

Lucy moved closer, her steps deliberate, symbolizing her support. The distance between them diminished, both physically and emotionally, as Jane's revelation bridged the gap of understanding, allowing Lucy a glimpse into the intricacies of emotions and memories that Jane was grappling with. The study, once a sanctuary for solitary reflection, transformed into a shared space of connection and empathy.

In this moment, the conversation between Jane and Lucy went beyond the exchange of information; it became a communion of souls, a joint exploration through the maze of past wounds and present obstacles. Surrounded by countless silent books, the study became a testament to the resilience of the human spirit, the capacity for empathy, and the enduring power of friendship. As Jane held the letter, a tangible link to her past, in the presence of Lucy, her confidant and ally in the present, their journey together deepened. The revelation that the mystery they were unraveling was entangled with Jane's own past added a poignant dimension to their quest, binding them closer in pursuit of truth and justice. In the soft dawn light, amidst the silent guardianship of the study, they stood at the threshold of understanding, ready to navigate the complexities of the human heart and the mysteries it holds. Sharing the letter's contents, Jane did more than recount a tale from her past; she opened a window into her soul for Lucy, unveiling the intricate ties that bound her to the darkness they sought to dispel. Each word read aloud was like a brushstroke on a canvas, painting a vivid picture of love, loss, and a past that refused to remain silent.

Lucy listened intently, her presence a steady beacon as Jane navigated her memories. The air in the study thickened with revelation, the morning light casting long shadows on the walls, mirroring the interplay of light and darkness within the narrative.

With an embrace that spoke volumes, Lucy offered solace—a physical manifestation of her unwavering support. "Oh, Jane. You're not alone. Whatever shadows we must face, we'll do so together," she affirmed, her voice a soft but resolute promise that pierced the solemn atmosphere. This embrace fortified the bond between them, a tangible reminder that no darkness was too profound to face when bolstered by the strength of friendship.

A fragile but sincere smile graced Jane's lips. "I know, and I'm thankful for you, Lucy. But some ghosts demand a reckoning, especially those entwined with secrets as dark as these." Her words acknowledged the complexity of the journey ahead. This exchange, set within Jane's study, was a testament to their shared resolve and the depth of their connection.

As they stood together, enveloped in the soft dawn light, Jane and Lucy were more than friends; they were allies in a battle against the shadows of the past. The study, with its countless books and artifacts, bore silent witness to this pivotal moment of unity and understanding. The challenges they faced were daunting, the path ahead uncertain, but the promise they shared—a promise of companionship and support—cast a light that no darkness could diminish. This window into Jane's soul, now shared with Lucy, transformed the letter from a mere artifact of the past into a catalyst for their collective future. Together, they stood at the threshold of a journey, not just to confront the ghosts that haunted them, but to forge a path illuminated by the strength of their bond and the unwavering light of hope.

Their moment of quiet reflection, a brief respite in the eye of an emotional storm, was interrupted by a knock at the door. This unassuming sound, laden with potential, signaled Alex's arrival. As the door swung open, revealing Alex framed by the doorway and holding a folder, the study was filled with a dim light that illuminated new insights. With an almost palpable anticipation, a silent promise of revelations that may be the key to navigating their investigation's labyrinthine paths.

"I've stumbled upon something – a piece of the puzzle that might help us weave through this tangled history," Alex announced, his voice blending excitement with the gravity of what he held. The folder, nondescript yet undeniably significant, seemed to glow in Alex's hands – a symbol of the hope and potential it represented. "Are you ready to confront the past head-on?" The question resonated in the air, challenging the newfound resolve that Jane and Lucy had just reaffirmed in each other's presence.

With a nod, reflecting her inner strength, Jane declared her readiness. "More than ready," she affirmed, her voice steady and fueled by the resolve forged from their shared experiences. "It's time we unravel this mystery, once and for all." Her words echoed decisively in the study, a space that had witnessed the ebb and flow of their journey, now standing as a testament to their determination to see it through to the end.

Standing by Jane's side, Lucy mirrored her determination, silently vowing unwavering support. The trio, united in purpose, stood on the precipice of discovery, weighed down by past encounters and unanswered questions that lingered in the shadows.

The study, lined with books and bathed in soft, diffused light, transformed into more than just a room – it became a crucible in which their path forward was forged. The air hummed with the potential of Alex's findings, and the folder in his hands became the key to unlocking the secrets that had eluded them. As they gathered around, getting ready to delve into the contents of Alex's folder, the study transformed into a command center for their final push against the darkness shrouding their mystery. Each piece of evidence, each clue held within, promised not only answers but also a confrontation with the very heart of the darkness they were determined to dispel. In this moment, surrounded by the silent witnesses of countless narratives encapsulated in the books that surrounded them, Jane, Lucy, and Alex stood ready to navigate through the tangled history that had bound them together. Their resolve shone like a beacon, cutting through the uncertainty of the journey that lay ahead.

Forming a circle of light in an otherwise dimly lit study, the trio gathered around the desk. The desk was cluttered with the artifacts of their investigation—photos, newspaper clippings, and now, Alex's folder. It became the epicenter not just of their physical evidence but also of Jane's personal history. It was a convergence of her past with their collective pursuit of truth, a task both daunting and sacred. The air in the room was thick with anticipation, each breath a testament to the weight of the moment. Jane's voice, contemplative and revealing a vulnerability seldom expressed, began to narrate their endeavor. "As we ventured deeper into the tangled threads of my own history," she started, her gaze fixed on the documents before them, yet seeing beyond, to the memories each piece evoked. "It became clear that the key to unlocking this enigma lay not solely in the tangible evidence at our fingertips, but also in the strength to face the remnants of a past marked by profound connection and loss." Her words, measured and reflective, filled the room, infusing their task with a sense of gravity.

The documents spread out before them were not just clues, but fragments of a life lived with passion and pain. Each item, each piece of paper, carried echoes of Jane's journey—a journey that had led her here, to this moment of reckoning with both her past and the shadow it cast over their present investigation.

Lucy, alternating her gaze between the documents and Jane, offered silent support, her presence a steady anchor in the tumultuous sea of revelations. Alex, with a keen eye, sifted through the evidence, their analytical mind piecing together the puzzle that was as emotional as it was factual.

Surrounded by the silent guardians of countless books, the room seemed to hold its breath as they delved deeper. The task ahead was layered with complexities—each discovery held the potential for revelation or heartache, each turn of the page brought them closer to understanding or served as a reminder of the loss that loomed over Jane's past. As they navigated through the complex history, their bond was undeniable, encompassing their shared determination to uncover the buried truths within Jane's story. The quest for justice, entwined with the need to confront the past, infused the study's atmosphere with a weighty solemnity that transcended the physical space.

In this serene enclave, surrounded by tangible manifestations of human thought and creativity, Jane, Lucy, and Alex were not merely investigators, but custodians of a narrative that demanded comprehension, reverence, and ultimate resolution. The odyssey through Jane's past, brimming with connection, grief, and the enduring resilience of the human spirit, exemplified their unwavering dedication to one another and their unwavering commitment to unearthing the truth, no matter how deeply it was buried.

Twilight Reflections: The Unfolding Path Ahead

NESTLED IN JANE'S SERENE garden, where the echoes of their recent hardships seemed to dissipate into the gentle rhythm of nature, Jane, Lucy, and Alex found much-needed solace. The chaos that had consumed their lives felt like distant whispers of the past, replaced by the harmonious chorus of the garden's inhabitants. The afternoon sun, casting a warm, golden glow, bathed them and created a flickering dance of light and shadow among the surrounding flora.

Seated around a modest table adorned with tea and the pleasure of each other's company, they quietly celebrated their survival and contemplated the future. The air carried the delicate fragrance of blooming flowers and the earthy scent of green, a testament to the garden's vibrant serenity.

Jane's voice, filled with reflection and newfound clarity, broke the comfortable silence that had settled amongst them. "In the aftermath of our ordeal, this tranquil moment reveals a profound truth—that every ending holds the potential for a fresh start." Her gaze wandered through the intricate patterns of light that graced the garden, finding symbolism in the natural beauty that embraced them. "Here, amid the serenity of nature's splendor, the promise of new beginnings feels not only possible but inevitable." Her soft yet resonant words encapsulated their collective respite, framing their experience as a transformative segment rather than the end of their story.

With a smile that mirrored the tranquility of their surroundings, Lucy reached across the table and gently squeezed Jane's hand, a gesture of unity and shared understanding. Alex leaned back in their chair, releasing a contented sigh, appreciating the strength and endurance reflected in the garden's vast expanse.

This moment, suspended in the golden haze of the afternoon, symbolized their journey—a journey that had plunged into darkness only to emerge into the light of understanding and renewal. The garden, with its unassuming beauty and steadfast growth, mirrored their own transformation, a reminder that even in the wake of chaos, life finds a way to thrive.

Sitting in the garden's embrace, the outside world beyond the hedges and blooms felt both distant and connected—a tapestry of untold stories. For Jane, Lucy, and Alex, the garden was more than an oasis; it was a beacon of hope, living proof that after every storm, opportunities for new beginnings, growth, and reimagination are possible. Lucy's spirit, buoyant after the passing storm, matched the serene atmosphere of the garden. With graceful elegance, she raised her cup, her smile blossoming like the vibrant flowers that surrounded them—a testament to resilience and the ability to find joy after sorrow. "To the paths we have traveled, to the bonds that have held strong through the tempest," she began, her voice warm like the sun that bathed them. "Here's to new beginnings, and to a friendship that endures beyond trials." Her heartfelt words, filled with shared experiences and the promise of the future, wove through the air, touching the hearts of her companions.

The clinking of their cups upon toasting Lucy's declaration created a delicate symphony that resonated in the tranquil garden. This simple yet profound sound sealed their shared resolve, affirming their collective journey and the new horizons that awaited them. The resonance of the glasses harmonized with the garden's natural symphony—the rustling leaves, the distant bird calls, and the soft murmur of the breeze.

In this moment, the garden transformed into a sanctuary of peace and renewal. Every detail, from the dappled sunlight to the gentle rustle of foliage, contributed to the sense of concluding one part and beginning another. Jane, Lucy, and Alex, surrounded by the beauty of the natural retreat, found strength in their fellowship and a reminder of the enduring power of connection.

The garden, a life-affirming presence, bore silent witness to their pledge and the resilience of their bond. It held the unspoken promise of countless tomorrows filled with growth, change, and continuing companionship. In this shared moment's tranquility, accentuated by the clinking of their cups, they were reminded that, though the journey might bring challenges, the true measure of their journey lay in the friendships that thrived amidst adversity, enduring like the steadfast garden that cradled their new beginnings.

With a mischievous grin that dissolved the remaining solemnity in the air, Jane added to the toast, her voice carrying a lighter tone tinged with mischief. "And to the hope that our next adventure might spare us from delving too deeply into our personal archives, hm?" Her playful remark, a gentle nudge toward the future, prompted shared laughter that mingled with the rustling leaves, adding to the garden's symphony of tranquility and rebirth. Alex, who had been silently supportive up until now, radiated a sense of calm amidst the chaos of their recent endeavors. Bathed in soft afternoon light, his features seemed almost otherworldly. His once contemplative eyes now blazed with curiosity and an insatiable desire for the unknown. "Speaking of adventures," Alex began, his voice a mix of intrigue and the determination that defined him, "there's a whisper of mystery on the outskirts of town—an enigmatic manor that holds legends, and perhaps, our next challenge." His suggestion lingered in the air, a tantalizing promise of unraveling secrets and stories yet to be unearthed.

The mention of a legendary manor sparked excitement in the group. The prospect of a new challenge, especially one steeped in history and the allure of the unknown, reignited their collective passion for uncovering hidden truths. The garden, once a haven for recovery and introspection, now brimmed with anticipation for what lay ahead.

Lucy, catching the infectious thrill of adventure, turned to Jane and Alex, her face lit up with the excitement of the hunt. "Well, it seems our respite will be shorter than we thought," she exclaimed, a vibrant eagerness to join her friends in unraveling another mystery evident in her voice.

In that moment, nestled in Jane's garden, bathed in the warm glow of the setting sun, the promise of a new adventure became a beacon of hope. It reminded them that their bond was built not only in adversity, but also in their unyielding pursuit of truth and their relentless curiosity.

As the garden surrendered to the encroaching shadows of evening, the trio stood on the brink of another journey. The serenity of the afternoon, the shared laughter, and the toast to new beginnings had all been a prelude to the next part of their story—one that would lead them from the tranquility of the garden to the enigmatic embrace of a manor cloaked in legends. The adventure that awaited them would test their resolve and further solidify the legacy they were creating together—a legacy of friendship, courage, and an unwavering quest for understanding in a world filled with enigmas.

Lucy's laughter, as light and carefree as the breeze that danced through Jane's garden, shattered the calm atmosphere that had settled over the trio. Her joy infused the air with a sense of buoyancy, a reminder of the happiness they found in pursuing their shared purpose. "It seems our break is short-lived," she announced, her eyes sparkling with excitement and a touch of mischief, acknowledging that they would soon have to return to their duties. "But with this fellowship, I welcome the unknown with open arms." Her words, spoken with genuine warmth and anticipation, were a testament to the strength of their bond, turning the prospect of facing the unknown from a daunting task into an eagerly awaited adventure.

Jane, joining in the laughter but wearing a contemplative expression, gazed out at the garden that had provided them solace. Her agreement was silent yet firm, a nod that conveys her eagerness to once again join her friends in their endeavors. "It appears that our small town holds more stories, waiting to be unraveled," she pondered, her voice soft yet carrying a strong undertone. The setting sun, casting long shadows across the lawn, seemed to reflect her thoughts - acknowledging the current tranquility while also promising the return of darker mysteries. "And honestly, I wouldn't have it any other way." Her statement, acknowledging their shared destiny, revealed her deeply held belief that their journey together, even though it was filled with dangers, was worth experiencing.

Alex, who had been quietly observing the conversation, offered a smile that was both wry and affectionate. His presence, steady and unwavering, silently affirmed his commitment to the cause and the companionship that had carried them through challenging times.

In that moment, the garden transformed from a simple backdrop to a sanctuary, offering a brief respite from the chaos of their mission. It reminded them of the beauty and peace that existed alongside the uncertainties they faced. As the last rays of the setting sun kissed the horizon, casting the garden into twilight, the promise of new adventures loomed large - a challenge they accepted, knowing that together, they were capable of conquering any mystery, no matter how daunting or dark. Their fellowship, formed in the face of adversity and fortified by unwavering loyalty and mutual respect, was their most powerful weapon against the unknowns that awaited them. With laughter, unspoken pledges, and the shared joy of discovery, Jane, Lucy, and Alex stood on the threshold of a new phase, ready to confront the secrets concealed within the manor on the outskirts of town. Guided by their indomitable spirits and the strength of their friendship, they were prepared to tackle whatever challenges lay ahead, embarking on their next adventure. As the afternoon sun slowly descended, casting elongated shadows across the garden, the trio became engrossed in the contours of the emerging mystery that called to them. The air surrounding them was thick with the golden hue of twilight, accentuating the serene yet charged atmosphere that enveloped their gathering. Their synergy was unmistakable, with their minds and spirits so in tune that the conclusion of one phase seamlessly paved the way for another. Their camaraderie, constant amidst the unpredictable ebb and flow of their endeavors, seemed to deepen with each shared glance and unspoken understanding.

Jane, leaning back in her chair with a contemplative gaze, surveyed the familiar and comforting confines of her garden, bringing a sense of closure mixed with anticipation. "The trials we've faced have only strengthened our bond, transforming our collective spirit in unimaginable ways," she began, her voice carrying the weight of their shared experiences and the depth of their unbreakable connection. Her eyes, reflecting the fading light, settled on Alex with a warmth that conveyed volumes. "Alex, now an essential part of our journey, has enriched our tapestry beyond measure." This acknowledgment was a testament to the evolution of their group, recognizing how each individual's strengths and vulnerabilities had interwoven to create a formidable force.

"The horizon may hold uncertainty," Jane continued, her gaze shifting to meet Lucy's, sharing a silent agreement that underscored the depth of their partnership. "Yet one conviction remains unshakable—we stand ready, united in purpose and spirit, for the adventures that lie ahead." Her declaration, infused with a resilience born from trials faced and overcome, served as a beacon of hope in the twilight of the day.

As the garden began to yield to the encroaching dusk, the vibrant colors of the flowers became muted in the fading light, yet their beauty remained undiminished—a metaphor for their own journey. The challenges they had encountered had not dimmed their resolve but had instead illuminated the strength of their bond and the unwavering spirit that propelled them forward.

As the sun dipped below the horizon, the garden was illuminated by a gentle, lingering glow, creating an atmosphere brimming with anticipation. This tranquil moment, a respite from the turbulent events of their recent history, served as a fleeting interlude in the grand symphony of their lives. Jane's poignant words resonated in their hearts, propelling them forward onto the precipice of the unknown, eager to embrace the enigmatic challenges that lay ahead. Their remarkable journey, defined by the trials they surmounted and their subsequent transformations, stood as a testament to the enduring strength of friendship, bravery, and an unwavering pursuit of truth in a world teeming with concealed mysteries yearning to be unraveled.

Under Starlit Skies: Reflections on Resilience and Renewal

IN THE HEART OF LAVENDER Lane, the town square pulsed with life as twilight washed the sky in soft hues. It became a vibrant tableau of community and celebration. The setting sun cast a golden glow, illuminating the faces of the townsfolk and the stalls adorned with local produce. Melodies floated through the air, interwoven like threads of gold, while laughter bubbled up like a clear spring. This painted a scene of collective resurgence from the shadows that once loomed over the town.

Jane gracefully moved through the square, her steps mirroring the buoyant atmosphere. She found herself captivated by the unfolding tapestry of life before her. Her voice, warm and filled with wonder, seemed to resonate with the very air itself as she narrated the scene. "There's a magic in the air when a community binds its wounds with unity and hope," she mused. Her eyes sparkled with the reflection of twinkle lights strung above the square. "Each smile, each burst of laughter, is a testament to the resilience of the human heart." Her words floated out, adding depth to the vibrant canvas of the evening.

The stalls were bursting with local craftsmanship and bounty. They showcased freshly baked goods in honeyed gold and handcrafted wares in a myriad of colors. Faces full of pride and joy tended to each stall, engaging in banter with the townsfolk. Good-natured humor and warmth underscored the sense of community that pulsed through the square like a heartbeat.

Lucy, walking alongside Jane, couldn't help but be swept up in the infectious joy of the scene. "It's as if the entire town has taken a deep breath and exhaled nothing but joy," she observed. Her laughter joined the symphony of sounds that filled the air. Her comment, light yet profound, captured the essence of transformation the town square embodied—a place of connection, healing, and rebirth, not just commerce.

As twilight deepened into night, the square took on a magical quality. Lanterns and twinkle lights cast a gentle glow, embracing the community. Local musicians lent their talents to the evening, creating a lively blend of music that invited dancing shadows to play across the cobblestones. This added a layer of whimsy to the celebration.

In this moment, with the soft twilight enveloping them and the vibrant life of the town square unfolding around them, Jane, Lucy, and the entire community of Lavender Lane were united in a celebration that went beyond the mere joy of festivity. It was a celebration of resilience, of the triumph of hope and unity over adversity, and of the indomitable spirit of a community that had stepped out of the shadows and into the light together. As Jane's gaze wandered through the vibrant throng of the town square, it inevitably found Lucy and Alex, their laughter and animated gestures making them a beacon of joy in the bustling crowd. Their presence seemed to draw people to them, as if their happiness was a gravitational force, pulling in those nearby with the promise of shared mirth and camaraderie. Approaching them, Jane's steps were light, almost dancing to the rhythm of the music that filled the air, her spirit buoyed by the palpable sense of renewal and unity that the celebration exuded.

With a playful reproach twinkling in her eyes, mirroring the fairy lights overhead, Jane greeted her friends, "A mere moment's absence, and you've woven yourselves into the fabric of local lore." Her voice, laced with amusement and affection, carried over the hum of conversations and melodies, drawing a delighted chuckle from Lucy and an amused raise of an eyebrow from Alex.

Turning to Jane with a wide smile, Lucy responded with mock solemnity, "It's our natural charm, I suppose. The town simply can't resist us." Her statement, delivered with a flourish, elicited a round of laughter from those nearby, further blending their small group into the communal tapestry of joy that the evening had woven.

Joining in the jest, Alex added, "We've merely been practicing our roles as Lavender Lane's newest legends. It's a tough job, but someone's got to do it." His comment, delivered with a perfect balance of sarcasm and warmth, underscored the ease and comfort that defined their friendship.

Around them, the square continued to pulse with life, a living mosaic of stories, laughter, and music. The trio, reunited in the heart of it all, shared a moment of connection that felt as deep and vast as the night sky above them. In this place, under the soft glow of twilight and amidst the echoes of a community reborn from the shadows, Jane, Lucy, and Alex found not just solace, but a profound sense of belonging. The evening unfolded around them like a shared dream, a moment suspended in time where the shadows of the past gave way to the light of present joy and the promise of future adventures. Here, in the heart of Lavender Lane, they were reminded of the enduring power of friendship, the resilience of their community, and the unwavering hope that danced like the lanterns in the gentle night breeze—a hope for tomorrow, for the stories yet to be told, and for the journeys yet to be undertaken.

Lucy's laughter, as infectious as ever, bubbled up and spread through their small circle, a light, melodious sound that seemed to capture the essence of the evening's joy. Her eyes sparkled with mirth and a touch of pride as she responded to Jane, "The tales of our little adventures seem to have captured their hearts." She swept her hand in a wide arc, gesturing to the vibrant crowd around them, each person a living thread in the tapestry of Lavender Lane's story. "But truly, Jane, have you ever witnessed the lane brimming with such vitality?" Her question, posed with genuine wonder, echoed the awe and appreciation that resonated with everyone gathered in the square. The lights, the laughter, and the shared sense of community painted a picture of a town not just revived but reborn, its spirit pulsating with newfound energy.

Alex, his gaze taking in the scene with thoughtful intensity, shared in the moment's reflective joy. "It feels as though we've all stepped together into a new phase," he mused, his voice carrying a note of optimism that seamlessly mingled with the evening air. "One where the past doesn't loom but instead informs a brighter path forward." His words, spoken with quiet conviction, captured the essence of transformation that hung palpably over the square. It was as if the trials and tribulations he had faced had been alchemized into the very foundation of his hope for the future—a future where the shadows of yesteryears served not as specters to fear but as milestones marking the journey toward light.

Around them, the town square thrived with the energy of a united community, each laugh and shared glance a testament to the enduring strength and resilience of Lavender Lane's inhabitants. The air was filled with possibility, the melodies that accompanied it a soundtrack to a collective step forward into a phase yet unwritten but already filled with promise.

Jane, Lucy, and Alex, standing together amidst the kaleidoscope of light and sound, found themselves not just participants in this communal rebirth but as catalysts who, through their courage and unwavering spirit, had helped guide their town out of the shadows. The vitality that Lucy marveled at, the new phase that Alex envisioned—it was all around them, a vibrant, living reality that they had helped shape. In this moment, beneath a sky washed in twilight hues, the lane not only brimmed with vitality; it overflowed with it. Each heartbeat in the crowd was a drumbeat heralding the dawn of a new era. An era where the past, with all its pain and lessons, seamlessly wove into the fabric of a future bright with the light of hope, unity, and enduring friendship.

Their exchange flowed, buoyed by the warmth and camaraderie that had defined their journey. It was graced by an unexpected yet welcome presence. The mayor, with a dignified air and a smile radiating genuine appreciation, joined their small circle. His gratitude was not just spoken but palpable—an aura that enveloped them, grounding the ethereal joy of the moment with the weight of recognition and respect.

"Your courage, your unwavering spirit, has gifted Lavender Lane not just with peace, but with a renewed sense of belonging and strength," the mayor began, his voice imbued with a depth of gratitude that resonated deeply with those gathered. "For that, we are eternally grateful." His sincere and heartfelt words bridged the space between leader and townsfolk, between gratitude and action, encapsulating the profound impact of their deeds on the fabric of the community.

Jane, ever embodiment of humility, responded with a grace that belied the depth of her contributions. "Our actions were but a reflection of the community's heart, Mr. Mayor," she replied, her voice soft yet firm—a gentle reminder of the collective effort that had steered Lavender Lane back into the light. "It's the spirit of the people here that truly defines Lavender Lane." Her response, while deflecting praise, underscored the interconnectedness of their actions with the larger tapestry of the town's resilience and heart.

The mayor, nodding in agreement, shared a look with Jane, Lucy, and Alex that spoke volumes. It was a look of mutual respect and a shared understanding of the strength derived from unity and the indomitable spirit of a community reborn. Around them, the town square, alive with the bustle of celebration and the vibrant tableau of community life, stood as a testament to the truth of Jane's words. The laughter, the music, the dance of lights and shadows—all were threads in the rich mosaic of Lavender Lane, each hue brighter, each note clearer, thanks to the courage and spirit of those willing to stand in defense of their home. In this moment, beneath the soft glow of twilight and the shared glow of accomplishment and gratitude, the exchange between the mayor and the trio was more than mere words of thanks. It was a recognition of the power of collective will and the transformative strength that comes from facing darkness together and emerging into the light stronger and more united. Lavender Lane, with its cobbled streets and bustling square, was more than just a backdrop to their exchange. It was a character in its own right, a witness to the trials and triumphs of its people, a beacon of hope, and a symbol of the enduring spirit of community.

As the mayor departed, leaving behind a trail of grateful acknowledgments and warm farewells, Jane's gaze was drawn away from the departing figure to a captivating sight at the heart of the square. There, amidst the laughter and light of the evening, stood a new addition—a mosaic that seemed to pulse with the vibrant colors of life itself. Each piece, meticulously placed, shimmered under the soft glow of the setting sun, creating a visual symphony of the community's journey from adversity to a unity that was as beautiful as it was unbreakable.

Approaching the artwork, Jane was momentarily lost in the intricate patterns and the depth of meaning held by each fragment. The mosaic, a kaleidoscope of hues and textures, seemed to tell a story not just of struggle but of triumph, of individual pieces coming together to form something greater than themselves—a symbol of the community's collective soul.

Gazing at the artwork with an expression of contemplation painting her features, Jane mused aloud, "This mosaic is a mirror to our collective soul—forged through challenges, yet standing testament to our interconnected strength and resilience." Her voice, soft yet filled with awe, echoed slightly in the cool evening air, capturing the essence of what the mosaic represented.

Lucy and Alex, drawn by Jane's reflective tone, joined her side, their eyes also tracing the dance of colors and shapes before them. Together, they stood in silent appreciation, allowing the mosaic to speak to them of trials weathered and victories shared, of the countless individual stories that, when woven together, formed the rich tapestry of Lavender Lane's identity.

The mosaic, in its silent eloquence, offered not just a reflection of the past but a beacon of hope for the future. Each piece, a testament to endurance and the transformative power of unity, shimmered with the promise that, no matter the darkness faced, the community could and would emerge stronger, more vibrant, and more united than ever before. In this moment, Jane, Lucy, and Alex found a renewed sense of purpose and a deepened appreciation for the bonds that held them. The mosaic, in its resplendent beauty, was more than just artwork. It was a declaration of resilience, a celebration of strength found in unity, and a profound reminder that together, they were capable of weathering any storm and emerging transformed.

Lucy stood beside Jane, taking a step closer to the mosaic. Her eyes traced the myriad pieces that told their collective story. The setting sun cast a warm glow on her face, highlighting the determination etched in her features. Turning to her friends, her voice, tinged with resolve, affirmed their unspoken pact. "It's a reminder that no matter what the future holds, we're prepared to face it together." Her words, spoken with quiet strength, resonated deeply, reinforcing the ties that bound them to each other and to the essence of Lavender Lane.

Alex, quietly observing the interplay of light on the mosaic, turned toward Jane and Lucy with a light-hearted grin. "Here's to future adventures—preferably ones that lean more toward celebration than peril." The humor in his voice brought forth laughter, a shared moment of levity that felt as vital as the air they breathed. His proposal carried an undercurrent of hope—a desire for a future where joy outweighed the shadows, where their gatherings could be marked by celebration rather than danger.

The laughter echoed around the square, blending with the evening's festivities, a testament to their enduring spirit. Around them, the town square, alive with community life, seemed to echo their sentiments. Each laugh, each note of music, was a building block in the foundation of their continued resilience.

Standing together in the fading light, the trio shared a look of understanding and anticipation. The mosaic before them, a beacon of their journey's past, now served as a stepping stone into a future ripe with possibilities. The promise of new adventures, of stories yet to unfold, hung in the air—a tantalizing horizon that beckoned them forward. In this moment, surrounded by the beauty of Lavender Lane and the warmth of their friendship, Jane, Lucy, and Alex found themselves not at an end, but at a beginning. The challenges they had faced had only served to fortify their resolve, deepen their connections, and prepare them for whatever lay ahead. With the mosaic as their witness and the square a canvas of their community's strength, they stepped into the twilight, ready for whatever adventures the future might hold - united in purpose and bound by an unbreakable spirit of camaraderie and hope.

Their laughter, vibrant and harmonious, seemed to rise and mingle with the evening's chorus - encapsulating the joy of a moment hard-earned. It was a sound that resonated beyond the confines of their circle, echoing the sentiment of a community reborn from adversity. The trials they had faced, while daunting, had not only fortified the bonds between Jane, Lucy, and Alex but had also woven their stories deeper into the vibrant tapestry of Lavender Lane. Their shared experiences, marked by both challenge and triumph, had become part of the larger narrative of the town's resilience and spirit.

As the vibrant hues of the evening yielded to the tranquil beauty of a star-studded night sky, the gathering around the square began to take on a reflective quality. The lights from the stalls and surrounding buildings twinkled like earthly reflections of the celestial splendor above - creating an atmosphere of serene contemplation.

In this moment of transition, as eventide merged into a canvas painted with stars, Jane found herself caught in a wave of introspection. Her closing thoughts, spoken softly yet with a clarity that cut through the gentle hum of the surrounding festivities, resonated with a profound truth. "The labyrinth we navigated revealed not the darkness we sought to vanquish but the enduring light of our collective spirit," she reflected, her voice a beacon in the growing dusk. "Our true journey was one of healing, of rediscovering the unbreakable hope that defines us." Her words hung in the air, a testament to the depth of their journey and the resilience it had unearthed.

Around them, the square - now bathed in the soft glow of twilight and the first stars of the evening - stood as a testament to the community's ability to face darkness and emerge stronger, more united. The laughter and music, the shared glances and quiet conversations - all spoke of a collective spirit rejuvenated by the trials it had overcome. Jane, Lucy, and Alex stood together under the starlit sky, not just as survivors of a dark phase in their town's history, but as symbols of hope and embodiments of the community's unwavering spirit. Their journey, filled with moments of fear and uncertainty, ultimately brought about a deeper understanding of themselves and their role within Lavender Lane.

Under the gentle embrace of the night, surrounded by signs of their community's strength and the tranquil beauty of a rejuvenated world, they discovered a sense of peace and purpose. The challenges they encountered were simply stepping stones on a path towards healing and self-discovery, shedding light on the everlasting hope and the power of unity. In this moment, under the watchful gaze of the stars, Jane, Lucy, and Alex stood as a testament to the enduring strength of friendship, resilience, and the indomitable hope that defines the human spirit.

Don't miss out!

Visit the website below and you can sign up to receive emails whenever S.R. Moore publishes a new book. There's no charge and no obligation.

https://books2read.com/r/B-A-XIBBB-MIDZC

BOOKS 2 READ

Connecting independent readers to independent writers.

Milton Keynes UK
Ingram Content Group UK Ltd.
UKHW020249290324
440307UK00017B/424